A GIRL
WALKS INTO
A BLIND DATE

A choose-your-own-erotic-destiny novel

Also in the
A Girl Walks in... series

A GIRL WALKS INTO A BAR

A GIRL WALKS INTO A WEDDING

A GIRL
WALKS INTO
A BLIND DATE

YOUR FANTASY,
YOUR RULES

Helena S. Paige

SPHERE

First published in Great Britain in 2014 by Sphere

Copyright © Sarah Lotz, Helen Moffett, Paige Nick 2014

The moral right of the authors has been asserted.

A CIP catalogue record for this book
is available from the British Library.

ISBN 978-0-7515-5258-4

Typeset in Sabon by M Rules
Printed and bound in Great Britain by
Clays Ltd, St Ives plc

Papers used by Sphere are from well-managed forests
and other responsible sources.

MIX
Paper from
responsible sources
FSC® C104740
www.fsc.org

Sphere
An imprint of
Little, Brown Book Group
100 Victoria Embankment
London EC4Y 0DY

An Hachette UK Company
www.hachette.co.uk

www.littlebrown.co.uk

A GIRL
WALKS INTO
A BLIND DATE

Every woman knows that internet dating is a lottery: you never know what kind of prize you're going to get. The sex god you've finally agreed to meet for coffee could be the stable, witty catch he's made himself out to be, but he's just as likely to be an out-of-work accountant with halitosis and three ex-wives.

You pour yourself a glass of wine and settle down with your laptop. You've dipped your toe in lovematch.com's murky waters before, with mixed results, and about a month ago you decided to give it one last try. After excluding the guys whose pictures were clearly ripped off bodybuilders' forums, and anyone who called themselves the 'world's bestest lover man', you narrowed your choices down to three. You've been chatting to them for a couple of weeks now – keeping it light – and so far, so good.

There's 'FireflyNYC', who says he's a fireman from New York City – two massive pluses in his favour. His profile pics are impressive, although you can't quite make out his face – they show a tall, hefty guy in a uniform and helmet, in the midst of scenes of derring-do.

1

He's made you laugh a few times and seems to genuinely love his job, but on the downside, his spelling isn't the greatest – usually a no-no for you. Plus, his favourite movies of all time are *An Affair to Remember* and *Taxi Driver*, which means he's either a closet romantic or a psychopath. Hmmm.

Then there's 'CountCanaletto36', who says he's descended from a long line of Venetian aristocrats and hails from 'the most beautiful city in the world'. His photographs show a tanned man with an aquiline profile and thick black hair – in one, he's leaning against the balcony of what looks like a gilded palazzo in Venice, and in another, he's wearing sunglasses and ski-gear against a snowy Alpine backdrop – and his messages are so beautifully written they're almost poetic. His interests include 'opera, literature and extreme sports', and he gives his occupation as 'entrepreneur'. He's confided in the course of some increasingly intimate chats that his real name is Count Claudio Lazzari, and you appreciate the trust implied. Sure, he still sounds way too good to be true, but you're not stupid – you've done some discreet online investigation, and he does indeed appear to be who he says he is.

And last but not least, there's 'LittleDutchBoy', a sculptor from Amsterdam. He's adventurous, quirky, and the word Bohemian could have been invented for him. It doesn't hurt that his pics show a cute guy with longish curly hair, and a very buff torso, but his English could use some help – sometimes when you're chatting to him, you get the impression you're in a relationship with Google Translate.

You log on, hoping you'll find a playmate, and you're pleased to see that all three of them have sent you messages. Maybe tonight should be the night to take things a little further. Who do you want to chat to first?

If you fancy some hot talk with the fireman, go to page 4.

If you're in the mood for the sexy sculptor, go to page 8.

For a little romantic banter with the aristocratic Italian, go to page 12.

You've decided to talk dirty with the fireman

Feeling slightly reckless, you ask Firefly if he'd like to take things a little further and, unsurprisingly, he's more than keen.

> <I've never done this before> you type.
> <Me niether>

Those typos could end up being a real passion killer. You'll just have to try to ignore them.

> <So ... how shall we start?>
> <U can tell me what yr wearing ... >

You're actually in your favourite flannel nightshirt, decorated with characters from *South Park* and ancient coffee stains. Not the sexiest outfit in the world. Time to lie.

> <A black, see-through fifties-style negligee and
> my favourite purple g-string. Oh! And high heels>
> <Mmmm. Purple is my favorite color>
> <Mine too>

Mine too? That's pathetic – surely you can do better than that. You think for a second, then type:

> <It's getting hot in here. Is it hot where you are?>
> <SO HOT>
> <How can I cool myself down? Do you have a hose I can borrow?>
> <Yeah, I do. U cn borrow it anytime, baby>
> <Is it big?>
> <HUGE. And if yr very good, I'll let you touch my helmet>

Fireman puns are just too easy. You can't really say this is turning you on, but it's fun.

> <I've always wanted to stroke a fireman's helmet. What does it feel like?>
> <It's hard, baby. Real hard. Like my POLE>
> You giggle. <Mmmm. Now I'm really getting hot>
> <You mite need to take something off>
> <I might. Oh look, I'm slowly lowering the straps of my negligee ...>

<Do it baby . . . do it slowly . . . >

<It's fallen on to the ground. All I'm wearing now is my g-string and heels. What should I do next?>

<Touch yr beasts>

You can't help it, you burst out laughing.

<My BEASTS?>

<Sorry. Got 2 excited!!! Forgot the R>

<It happens>

<Yeah. Still LOLing>

LOLing? Oh dear, but you type:

<Me too ☺!>

<Wait. Brb>

He's back online in thirty seconds.

<Gotta go. Rain chek???>

<Sure. And be safe out there>

<U 2 XXXX>

That was amusing rather than erotic, and although you hope he might be a bit more articulate in person than online, at least he has a sense of humour. Plus you're getting used to the poor spelling. What to do now?

To chat to the sculptor, go to page 8.
To message the Count, go to page 12.
To call it a night, go to page 19.

You've decided to chat to the sculptor

Online flirting is going to be something of a challenge via Google Translate, but what the hell, you think – you'll try anything once.

> <So, how's Amsterdam tonight?> you type.
> <Amsterdam is a beautiful city>
> <I hear it's also a very sexy city ... >
> <It would be more sexy if you are here>

Now we're talking, you think, beginning to feel a little flushed.

> <How do you know? You've never even met me>
> <You sound sexy>
> <You've never heard me either>
> <I am artist. I do not hear to know that you are sexy. I have imagination>
> <Is that so? And do you imagine me often?>
> <Yes, if I say the truth. I imagined the night before, you were here>

You type a response, feel shy, delete it, retype it, and then press 'enter' before you can change your mind again:

> <And what were you imagining?>
> <I imagining that you were here and we kissed>
> <Really? And was I a good kisser?>
> <Yes very well. Almost as well as myself>

You laugh. There's nothing sexier than a man with a sense of humour. Even in the weird world of Google Translate, he's funny.

> <Well ... maybe you could give me some lessons?>

Mmm. He could give you kissing lessons, and you could give him English lessons ...

> <I would like>
> <I think I'd like more>
> <And in my imagining, when we were done with kisses, I let my hand go into your panties and fingered you to coming>

You swallow. This is getting serious. Heat rushes through your body, and you wriggle a little, letting your own fingers wander down south.

> <you hav a verry vivid inagimation>
> <Are you now touching yourself?>
> <what makess you say that>
> <I'm here the one who has bad English, so I think you must be typing with one hand only>

Caught out, you snap both hands on to the keyboard, trying to decide how to respond. You're flushed, partly from embarrassment and partly from arousal. How do you answer? You don't want to tell him the truth – that just a few words from him has you fiddling in your drawers. Mercifully, he notices your long pause and comes to your rescue by changing the subject.

> <Maybe you should just come to Amsterdam, then we no longer have to make a fantasy>
> <Maybe ... > you type. And then you add <maybe ... > again.

Your computer pings as a chat request comes in from someone else.

> <Maybe you should not perhaps come, but definitely>
> <It's definitely a maybe>

You'll leave him to figure out that phrase on his own.

> <Thanks for the chat, sexy boy. Talk again soon. xxx>

You log out quickly before he can suck you back in, and check your inbox – there's a new message from the Count, and one from Firefly too. Do you respond, or have you had your fill of juicy banter for one night?

To chat to the fireman, go to page 4.
To message the Count, go to page 12.
To call it a night, go to page 19.

You've decided to chat to the Count

<Ciao bella!> comes the Count's usual
greeting, and you tell him it's great to hear
from him, wondering whether it would be
cheesy to send one of those kiss-wink
emoticons that indicates 'I'm feeling flirty'.

As if your thoughts are being transmitted through
the cyber-ether, he types:

<I have something to ask you tonight>

Ooh. This sounds promising.

<Anything you like!> you respond.
<May I be very bold? May I picture you
naked?>

You gulp a bit. But you have to admit, you're keen
on the idea – and what harm can it do?

<Er, sure, go ahead. But be warned, I might be
picturing stuff too>

12

> <Those beautiful breasts. I am sure the skin is
> as soft and smooth as cream. Right now, I am
> imagining strawberries with my cream.
> Cherries. Wait, grapes! Plump and firm and ripe
> on my tongue . . .>

Your nipples have leapt to attention at his words. You slide a hand inside your top and click over to his photo, admiring his sensual mouth, the strong shape of the bow of his top lip, the glint of white teeth. You imagine that mouth travelling down the bare skin of your chest, kissing its way over your breasts, capturing your nipples. Your breath starts coming a little faster, and your hand trails down to play with one of your breasts, rolling the nipple gently between your fingertips.

> <Is that all right? I haven't offended? Must I
> stop?>
> <No!>
> <Good, so you like?>
> <Um yes>

You can't wait to see where this will lead. You're a bit nervous – you know all about cyber-sex, but you've never actually tried it. So far, you're mostly intrigued – and more than a little turned on.

> <I need to taste more of this cream>
>
> <Be my guest>
>
> <Lapping, like a cat. Ah, you taste so good, you are so sweet and sexy, all at the same time . . . >
>
> <Thanks, you're pretty sexy too>
>
> <So you are enjoying this? Me, I am enjoying it very much. And shall I tell you what I enjoy even more?>
>
> <Go ahead!>
>
> <Figs>
>
> <???>
>
> <They are my favourite. I am thinking how much I like to run my thumb down the tender skin, peeling it apart, opening up the fruit . . . >

Heat flushes through you as the penny drops, and a thrill surges through your pussy. Hastily, you type back <wow> with one hand as you shift your laptop aside and tug down your cotton knickers. You take another quick look at his profile pic, and this time you imagine his mouth travelling south. Giving a little moan at the thought of those firm lips ministering to your tropical zones, you adjust the pillows behind you and let your knees fall apart. Meanwhile, Claudio is still typing:

<to expose the soft deep pink flesh, the
juice ... >

And you can't resist, your own fingers slip down to your thighs, your middle finger curling in to part your pussy lips, which are swollen and damp. Between them, you're certainly as juicy as Claudio is imagining ...

<i like to split the fig wide open, and then eat
the inside, pressing it into my mouth, using my
tongue to catch every drop>

You whimper, shamelessly stroking your pussy, running your finger up from the wet opening to your clit as you watch the screen, anticipating the little 'ping' sound that accompanies each line of chat.

<figs and cream, the perfect combination>
<yss> you type, not very accurately.

Fortunately, Claudio (who, you notice, has abandoned the use of capital letters) is too much of a gentleman to comment.

<i especially like the dark, musky figs>

And then, a few seconds later:

<so succulent ripe>

You're beyond typing, helplessly massaging your clit, feeling the sense of urgency growing in your soaking pussy, the ache deep in your pelvis demanding relief.

<I lick the delicate inner skin>
<then I go back for more>

As his words appear on the screen, you tip over the edge, coming in a glorious flood, your body bending like a bow against your pillows. Your laptop slides off the duvet, but you're enjoying yourself too much to care. Pleasure radiates through your body, and for a few long seconds, it really feels as if Claudio's right there with you, and that he's just given you a fabulously satisfying orgasm.

You realise that's exactly what has happened – in a manner of speaking – and scrabble for your laptop. Fortunately, you haven't accidentally switched it off, or exited the program, and there are several messages waiting for you in the chat window:

<but perhaps this is enough for you>

<bella?>

<I hope I have not gone too far?>

<no no> you type hastily. <that was really really great>

<Ah, I trust you are satisfied? I know I am>

You blush. And then stretch, knitting your hands until your knuckles crack.

<Mmmm. Let's say I'll sleep well tonight>

<In which case, let me kiss you goodnight and wish you good dreams. Of me, I hope. Xxx>

You smile and type back <xxxx>. You always thought cyber-sex might be a bit impersonal, even tacky, but it was surprisingly romantic. And very, very hot. It certainly hit the spot … You pad off to run a bath, still grinning.

Go to page 19.

You've decided to call it a night

Well, that was interesting. You have a luxurious bath, make yourself some cocoa and are about to head off to bed when your laptop beeps yet again. There are three messages waiting for you from lovematch.com.

The first is from the sculptor:

<Perhaps it is the time that we get together?>

The second is from the Count:

<Bella, I feel a great longing to see your beautiful face in person>

And the third is from FireflyNYC:

<Hey. Wanna meet IRL?>

Wow. What are the chances of all three of them coming up with the same idea? And what should you do now? You've got your bonus from work, and you could easily take some time off. But are you really going to fly off and meet a relative stranger in an unknown city?

You mull it over. Worst-case scenario, if you go to New York and it doesn't work out with Firefly, you can always do some shopping, see the sights and soak up the atmosphere. And who doesn't want to explore Venice? Even Venetians like to go there for their holidays. Then there's Amsterdam: everything you've heard about it suggests you could be in for a wild ride – on a bicycle, if that's your choice.

Decisions, decisions …

If you'd like to go Dutch and visit your sculptor, go to page 21.
If you decide to count in the Count, go to page 113.
If you take up Firefly's offer, go to page 245.

You've decided to go to Amsterdam to see the sculptor

You type:

> <You're on! I've decided to come to
> Amsterdam!>

LittleDutchBoy's message blips on to the screen almost the second you've pressed 'enter'.

> <Fantastical! When you are coming?>

As soon as possible, you think, but you decide not to type that. You quickly Google flights. There's a reasonably priced one leaving in a couple of days. You send him the details.

> <I am send you my address now, also my
> name, which is Sven!> he responds. <See you
> coming soon!! XXX>

You smile. At least the letter X can't get lost in translation.

21

You open a new page to search for 'boutique hotels, Amsterdam', but as you scroll down, you accidentally click on one of the ads in the side bar. A window pops open and 'Kink's Online Boudoir' flashes before your eyes. Curious, you scroll down the page. You're not a complete stranger to sex toys. Someone once gave you a vibrator for a gag birthday gift, and it's been a close friend on and off, ever since. But you've never actually been in a sex shop, or bought anything fancier than a little playful lubricant or condoms from your local pharmacy.

Three items catch your eye as you navigate the site. The first is a white latex nurse's outfit. Its skin-tight boned bodice laces up the back with a red silk ribbon, and its skirt is so short, there would be very little polite sitting-down in it. It also comes with white fishnet stockings, red patent-leather stilettos that make you want to click your heels twice and say 'there's no place like home', a headpiece with the obligatory red cross decal, and a pair of barely-there knickers that on closer inspection are almost entirely crotchless.

Hey, if meeting LittleDutchBoy for the first time

gets awkward, you should be able to kiss and make it all better in this get-up.

The next item that catches your eye is billed as a 'Starter Bondage Kit'. Bondage isn't something you've ever tried before, but then you've never booked a flight to meet a blind date before either, so it appears that this is turning into a day for trying out new things. The kit contains a pair of handcuffs that look like the real thing, a black leather whip with a number of knotted tails, a riding-crop, and a rather ridiculous black leather mask with a zip for a mouth. Sven may not be able to speak perfect English, and your Dutch is non-existent, but surely neither of you will have any problem understanding the universal language of spanky-spanky?

You scroll down further and lean in for a closer look at a purple trinket. It's a bullet-shaped ornament with a small wireless remote control, like a garage-door clicker. According to the blurb, it's a 'Remote Control Love Egg'. The vibrating bullet goes into your pussy, and whoever has the remote control chooses the level, intensity and duration of the vibrations. Imagine the possibilities.

You should definitely get a little saucy something to

take with you. You don't have to use it if you don't want to, but what fun if you do. The only question is: which item should you pick?

If you pick the naughty nurse's outfit, go to page 25.
If you pick the starter bondage kit, go to page 29.
If you pick the remote-controlled bullet, go to page 58.

You've picked the naughty nurse's outfit

Your mouse hovers over 'add to basket': you take a deep breath and click. The details page appears asking where you want your outfit delivered. You're about to fill in your home address when a better idea pops into your head. You could have it sent directly to Sven with a suggestive note written with the kind assistance of Google Translate. You do the maths. They offer a twenty-four-hour courier service, so the package should arrive at his place tomorrow, giving him a taste of what's to come. It's such a cute little outfit, what red-blooded man wouldn't find it tantalising?

You fish around for the scrap of paper on which you've copied down his address, tap it in, add your credit card details, and agree to the terms and conditions. Then you type a quick note:

Dear Sven,

I'm looking forward to meeting you in the flesh.

I know this is a little kinky, but I thought this

outfit would be a great way to break the ice. I

hope you like it?

See you soon.

X

With the help of Google Translate, it becomes:

Geachte Sven,
Ik kijk er naar uit u te ontmoeten in het vlees. Ik
weet dat dit een beetje kinky, maar ik dacht dat
dit outfit zou een geweldige manier om het ijs
te brekenzijn. Ik hoop dat je het leuk?
Tot snel weerziens.

X

You copy and paste it into the field provided and click 'send'. This is going to be one blind date neither of you will ever forget. Then you haul out your suitcase. That's your first holiday outfit sorted, and while you don't plan on wearing too many clothes while you're in Amsterdam, you should probably pack a few other items, just in case.

You're hunting for your passport the next morning, when you hear the ping of a message landing in your inbox. You've been hovering around your laptop, waiting for a response to your note, grinning as you imagine the look on Sven's face when the gift arrives.

Yes, it's from him! Feeling a tingle in your nether regions, you hesitate before opening the message to prolong the anticipation. How can you be this hot and bothered just thinking of someone you've never even met? It must be the thought of all the things he's going to do to you with those sculptor hands of his. Unable to resist any longer, you open his message. You're surprised – it's in Dutch, and he usually translates his messages first. You quickly cut and paste it into Google Translate.

> Your parcel arrived today.
> The contents surprised me somewhat.
> I think it is wise to tell you that I am here not like you.
> So maybe we're coming to Amsterdam better move to a later time.
> I am currently also working on because a new job, so it does not look so good to you now to see Amsterdam.
> I have your Gimp Suit returned to sender.

I hope you find what you are looking for.

Sven

Your cheeks burn fuchsia. A gimp suit? What's he talking about? The online sex shop must have delivered the wrong package. With the language barrier, how can you even begin to explain the mistake to him? And even if you could, would you ever be able to look him in the eye? What a disaster.

Your computer pings again. You shudder, hoping it's not Sven, and peek at the screen through your fingers. Thankfully, it's a message from Firefly, just dropping by to say 'hi'.

Hmmm. Maybe you don't have to cancel your trip after all: you could just pick another location – and who doesn't love a New York fireman? Then there's the lure of your aristocratic playboy in Italy ... you've always wanted to go to Venice. You know what they say about one door closing ...

To go to Venice to visit the Count, go to page 113.

To go to New York City to check out the fireman, go to page 245.

You've picked the starter bondage kit

You shuffle forward in the queue, your ticket and passport in hand. You can't believe you're doing this! Who jumps on a plane to go on a blind date? Clearly you do. Your heart thumps at the prospect of what the next few days might hold. After you've arrived and located your hotel, the first thing you're planning on doing is telling Sven that you've arrived safely. Then maybe dinner together – and after that, who knows?

You clutch your carry-on bag closer. As well as the usual travel paraphernalia, it contains a new book, spare underwear and your starter bondage kit. You were going to bury it at the bottom of your suitcase, but what if it got lost in transit and officials had to open your case to identify the owner? You'd be far too embarrassed to claim it back, so you decided to take the kit on board with you instead.

You're so busy daydreaming, you step through the metal detector frame without putting your bag on the conveyor belt. There's a high-pitched beeping sound, and you're ushered sternly back through to the other side.

'Shoes,' a gruff security guard barks at you.

You take them off and drop them into the tray with your bag.

'Belt.'

You remove that too, then walk back through the metal detector. Sirens blare, lights flash and you're instantly descended on by several more security guards. You do a quick mental body search. What could have set off the machines this time? Your necklace, or perhaps the wire in your bra?

But it's not you, it's your bag. Uh-oh. Your throat feels like you're swallowing an acorn. A female guard frisks you while two others whip through your bag. One pulls out the handcuffs, blinks, and then glares at you. The other is staring at the knotted whip and – oh, the horror – the zip-up mask. It dawns on you that the passengers in the neighbouring queues are staring at you with a mixture of shock and glee – it looks like you've scored yourself a starring role in hundreds of future travelling anecdotes, along with a couple of Instagram and Facebook posts.

The airport security interrogation room contains nothing but a metal table, two chairs and a camera on a tripod in the corner. A small red light on it blinks as you shift in your seat. A million thoughts race through your mind. How exactly are you going to explain this? Will you be arrested? And are you going to make your flight?

After what feels like an age, the door opens, a man steps inside, and there's a subtle shift in the atmosphere. You're not sure what you were expecting, but this isn't it. This guy is tall, with broad shoulders, and dark-brown hair. He's wearing a pair of tightly fitting jeans, a checked shirt and black boots. He looks more like a rugged TV soap star named Ridge, Twig or Storm than an airport official.

'Sorry to have kept you waiting,' he says, flipping open your passport, and comparing you with your photograph. You wince; to say it's an unflattering likeness is an understatement. It looks like a mug-shot, which won't help your cause here.

He catches your eye, and it might just be you, but is that a tiny zing of chemistry between you? He has a square jaw and perfectly white teeth, and the blue of his eyes is made even deeper by long black eyelashes. You glance down at his hands. They're larger than average (and no wedding ring). You cast a quick look at his Timberland boots – also larger than average.

'Aren't you security guys supposed to be in uniform?' you blurt.

He assesses you for a long moment. 'This is my uniform,' he says. 'I usually work undercover. I get called in to deal with the more … unusual cases.'

'Oh.'

'So, let's see what we have here,' he says, dropping your bag on the table.

A flush races up your neck to your cheeks. 'There's been a terrible mix-up …' you stutter. 'I'm not … it's not …'

He unzips your bag, and the first thing he pulls out is a black lace g-string. He folds it professionally without making eye contact and returns it to your bag, then he slowly unpacks and places each offending item on the table, noting them down on his clipboard as he does so.

'Handcuffs, police issue. Large whip. Small whip …'

You slide down as far as you can in your seat, wishing the floor would open up and swallow you.

'... and maybe you'd like to explain this?' he asks, holding up the mask.

'It's freezing in Amsterdam at this time of year,' you say.

He takes the seat across from you, his expression serious. 'You can see how bad this looks, can't you?' he says.

You nod, unable to find your voice.

'We take matters of international security extremely seriously ...'

'I'm not a terrorist!' you squeak, fear ripping through you, as visions of yourself in a cell in Guantánamo Bay spring to mind. You clearly watch far too much late-night television.

'It's okay,' he says, his voice gentler. 'We didn't think you were.' A small smile cracks the corners of his lips. This man should be playing a security agent on TV, instead of being one in real life. He's far too good-looking for this.

'You didn't?' you say, limp with relief.

'We just needed to be certain. I'm sure you understand. Anyway, we've checked you out, and you're free to go.'

'Oh thank God!' you say.

He smiles again, and hands you your bag, so you can pack your things away. You reach for the larger of the two whips and hastily shove it out of sight.

'I've never done anything like this before, you know,' you babble.

'That's what they all say,' he says as he gets up and turns off the camera.

'I really haven't, I swear, cross my heart and hope to die.'

'Well, in that case, I am a little worried.'

'You are?'

'Yes, these items can be quite dangerous if you don't know what you're doing.' He dangles the handcuffs from the tip of a finger. 'I wouldn't want you to hurt yourself, or anyone else for that matter.' His eyes are sparkling. 'I could show you how some of this stuff works, if you want.'

'You would do that?' you say. You stare at him. Can he possibly mean what you think he means?

'Sure. It's pretty much my civic duty. I have a lot of experience with this stuff.'

'You do?'

'I'm a security agent, remember.'

You glance at your watch; if you hurry, you could

still catch your flight. Not to mention that Sven is waiting for you at the other end of your journey. Or do you have the perfect blind date standing right in front of you, looking at you with come-to-bed eyes and offering to teach you a couple of his tricks? Why cram yourself on to a plane, to get to something that's right in front of you?

If you stick around with the security agent, go to page 36.
If you run to catch your flight, go to page 44.

'So, the handcuffs are pretty easy to operate,' he says, holding them up. 'These are standard issue. The secret is to make sure you don't ever lose the key. That would be awkward.'

You wonder if he's joking to cover up a touch of excitement. You can relate: your heart is fluttering a mile a minute in your chest as you perch on the table in front of him. If you're going to miss your flight for this guy, you might as well make it worth your while.

'You just close them like this,' he says, clicking one of the segments into the other. 'See, easy.' Then he unlocks them again, showing you how.

'I'm not sure I fully understand. Perhaps if you show me how they work on me, I'll get a better idea,' you say, holding your hands out in front of you, an innocent look on your face.

You hear his breath catch. 'Here? Now?'

'Well, you said so yourself, I could hurt someone if I don't know how to use this stuff properly. Unless you have somewhere else you need to be?'

'I think this is a priority. We take safety extremely seriously round here,' he says, stepping over to the door and locking it.

Then he comes over to you and loops his fingers around your wrists, his thumb and forefinger touching. 'You wrap the handcuff around the wrist like so, and lock the arm into the slot.'

'I'm still not sure I get it,' you say, and he's close to you now, so you speak softly. 'Perhaps you'd better show me again.'

'Stand up,' he instructs, his voice low and strict. Slowly you slide off the desk on to your feet, which brings you very close to him. 'First I need to frisk you, to make sure you're not carrying anything dangerous.'

You don't move, a little unsure what he expects from you.

He takes your arm and leads you towards the wall, and you get it – you know the drill, you've watched enough police dramas on TV. You face the wall, placing your hands flat against it. You can't resist looking over your shoulder at him and smiling, and he growls, 'Spread 'em!', but with an answering smile. He uses one foot to gently nudge and then tap at the inside of your shoe, and you spread your legs wide, your breath coming faster now.

He pats you down, starting with your arms, the warmth of his breath on your neck as he feels along your shoulders and then down the length of your arms. Goosebumps rise along your bare arms as he strokes down them, his fingers sure. He returns to your neck, but this time he runs his hands down your front from behind, patting gently across your collarbone and then skimming over your breasts, your nipples hardening instantly at his touch. Then he runs his hands down your sides, and along the front of the waistband of your skirt, sliding his thumbs in between your skirt and your skin, just flirting over the lace edging of your panties.

All too soon, he abandons your front and squats behind you, running both hands all the way down one leg, then all the way back up again, then moving to your other leg, his hand brushing the scrap of fabric between your thighs. As he runs his hands down to your ankles, you have to close your eyes and focus to stop yourself from begging him to return to the spot between your legs.

He stands, and without saying a word, turns you to

face him, then runs his hands up your arms, pushing your wrists up against the wall behind you, pinning you against the wall.

'Your skin is amazing,' he growls in your ear. The urge to lean forward and kiss him is potent. This is a complete stranger, you think. I should be getting on a plane to Amsterdam right now. You breathe in, and you can smell him, all male. Holding both your wrists in one hand above your head, he runs his thumb along the line of your jaw.

Then he kisses you at last, running his hand down your back and on to your bum, pulling you even closer into him, his cock pressing against you, hard and insistent. Then he steps back.

'You've been a bad girl, haven't you?' he says.

'I'm afraid so,' you say meekly, holding out one arm to him. He puts one handcuff around your wrist, the metal cold against your skin. There's a steely click.

'I see,' you say. 'So they work like this?' And before he can react, you take the other cuff and snap it on to his wrist. 'Oops,' you murmur. 'Now, where did I put that key?'

His eyes flare, possibly with alarm, but you're hoping it's lust. 'So we're inextricably linked,' he says, shuffling back over to the table with you. You lean on the edge, facing him, eager to see what he does next.

Holding your eyes, he runs the finger of his free hand down your cheek, slowly along your neck, down to the opening of your blouse. When he reaches the first button, he tweaks it open with that single finger, then trails down to the second button, opening that too. He keeps going, taking his time, teasing you, until your blouse is unbuttoned all the way. He pulls it open and eases one breast out of the cup of your bra, then runs his tongue over your nipple. You groan as he pinches your nipple, then blows on it gently before licking it again. The contrasts – his hard fingers, his soft tongue, his breath, cool on your burning skin – have you wriggling.

He moves back to your shoulders, alternating small sharp bites and gentle sucking – you're sure the bites are going to leave marks, and the thought of having reminders of their infliction makes you even hungrier.

At last his hand slides up your thigh, nudging under your skirt, and you shiver, eager for more. He leans in and kisses you again as his thumb finds your pussy, probing gently. You squirm, trying to pull him closer, finding yourself thwarted by the handcuff linking your arms, but there's something delicious in the frustration of not getting what you really want – scratch that, what you really need.

'Just one more question, ma'am,' he pants in your ear. 'Is this what you really want?'

'Yes,' you whisper.

'Like this?' he asks, darting a finger inside you, making you groan.

'More,' you gasp, and he slips a second finger inside you, finding a rhythm, and you bend back on your arms as he makes you come quickly. Then he spreads your thighs as you half-lean, half-sit against the table, your head spinning, drops down and starts to lick your pussy, his hand, shackled to yours, planted on your thigh. You're shuddering, your post-orgasmic pussy almost unbearably sensitive, but he avoids your clit and focuses on your opening, darting his tongue in and out, until your moans rise again – it's almost too much.

As if he senses you're feeling overwhelmed, he rises to his feet, the hand locked to yours grasping for and meshing with your fingers, and kisses you hard. You lose yourself in his feel of his mouth, but he hasn't forgotten your pussy, and he presses his knee gently but rhythmically against it as he kisses you. His free hand roves your body, squeezing your breasts, tweaking your nipples, and then he sinks down again, his mouth back on and in your cunt, lapping at you, sucking at you, making you pulse and reel.

'Oh dear God,' you say, feeling his tongue and now his fingers in the very depths of you again, and at last he zeroes in on your clit, and all the sensations cluster together, promising a fierce orgasm. This time you come quietly, but two fat tears squeeze out of your eyes and roll down your cheeks.

When you're back on the planet, he straightens up, and wipes away one of your tears. There's a long pause, then he asks: 'You were kidding about not knowing where the handcuff key is, right?'

You wrap your free arm around his neck, giggling, but you're too lazy and satisfied to tease him. 'It's in my bag, side pocket.'

He stretches for it, then fumbles for your wrist, and you hear a click. You're both free, and he's rubbing your wrist where the cold metal encircled it. 'One down, two to go,' he says.

'Two?'

He indicates the two whips on the table.

42

'What about that?' you say, pointing out the third and final item – the mask.

'We won't be needing that,' he says, reaching for you. 'I think we'll be more than warm enough. Plus we have a lot of business to whip through tonight.'

THE END

'If I hurry, I can still make my flight,' you say, glancing at your watch, gathering your bits and pieces together and shoving them into your bag. He's cute, but what are you going to do, shag him in the interview room? Anyway, the excitements of Amsterdam and LittleDutchBoy (aka Sven) await.

He holds up the handcuffs: 'I'm afraid you can't take these on the plane with you – it's against airline regulations.'

'Promise you'll take good care of them?'

'You have my word,' he says, with a slow smile.

Just before you leave, he hands you the mask. 'You'd better take this. I wouldn't want you to get cold.'

You can't help laughing as you make a dash for the departure gate, your overnight bag slightly lighter than it was forty-five minutes ago.

You're relieved to make it to the gate on time, and even more relieved to discover your flight isn't that full. As you struggle to lodge your bag into the overhead compartment, the man behind you stops to help.

At least chivalry isn't dead. You admire his biceps as he raises your bag over his head, and his shirt lifts to show a slice of the smooth, tanned skin of his abdomen, along with a silken trail of hairs dipping down into the waistband of his jeans. He registers you checking him out, and you blush, thank him, then get into your seat so he can pass down the aisle.

'Actually, that's me,' he says, indicating the window seat one over from you. Of course it is! You step back out into the aisle and let him slide past you. Then you settle into your own seat, stealing glances at him, a pleasurable glow settling in your chest when the seat between you remains empty. The captain's voice crackles over the intercom, informing you that the flight will be delayed on the ground due to fog, and you exchange eye-rolls with your neighbour. 'Hope you're not in a hurry to get there,' he says.

You shrug. 'Nothing too urgent.'

'Business or pleasure?' he asks.

'As much pleasure as I can squeeze in,' you say. 'You?'

'Business.'

'Wait, let me guess, you're an astronaut?'

He laughs, which lights up his face.

45

'Okay, okay,' you say. 'Trapeze artist?'

He laughs again, shaking his head.

'Stuntman? Glass blower? Rocket scientist?'

'Architect.'

'That was going to be my next guess, I swear!' you say.

'So, is your husband not travelling with you?' he asks, which you know is international code for: are you single?

'No husband,' you say, holding up your bare ring finger and wiggling it. 'What about you? Doesn't your wife or girlfriend mind you going away on business without her?'

'Nope, neither of them mind,' he says with a cheeky grin.

The delay has continued for so long, the crew has decided to serve drinks to keep the passengers happy. But conversation with your neighbour flows so smoothly, you're barely aware of time passing. You've both covered your basic CVs and you've learned that your new friend's name is Ryan, he's on his way to a conference, he likes rock climbing and travel, and there's something inexplicably sexy about the crease of his eyes when he smiles. He didn't tell you that part – you came to that conclusion all by yourself.

Dinner is served, he has the steak, you have the chicken, he gives you his olives, and you both leave the green peppers, agreeing that they're the devil's work.

'We'd better finish this,' Ryan says, tapping the miniature wine bottle.

'Dinner, wine … if we weren't strapped to chairs in a large metal box, this would feel an awful lot like a date,' you say, holding your cup out so he can top it up.

'Yes, but to clarify, if I were to go on a date with you, I promise I wouldn't take you anywhere with plastic cups.'

Finally the captain announces that the plane will be taking off in the next ten minutes. The flight attendant clears your trays, the lights in the cabin dim for take-off, and as the plane begins its taxi down the runway, you unravel your headphones and plug them in. You tap around the touch screen, pick something arbitrary and press 'play'. But there's no sound. You prod at the buttons and turn the sound all the way up – still nothing.

'I'm happy to share, if you like,' your neighbour says, disconnecting a pair of earphones from his iPod. 'The audio will be much better through these anyway.'

If you'd rather read your book, go to page 49.
If you want to share headphones, go to page 50.

'That's kind of you, thanks. But I think I'm just going to read my book,' you say, reaching into the pocket of the bag by your feet.

'What are you reading?' he asks.

'I haven't started it yet. It's called *A Girl Walks into a Blind Date*.' You flash the cover at him.

'Well, enjoy it,' he says.

'I think I'm going to,' you say, leaning back and cracking the spine as you open it. There's nothing better than the exciting possibilities of a new book.

Go to page 1.

As soon as the seatbelt lights ping off, Ryan shuffles over into the seat beside yours, and there's a little spark at his proximity.

'Dinner and a movie,' he says, 'now it really is a proper date.'

He raises the armrest between you, and you're aware of the warmth of his body.

'So, what's it going to be, rom-com, action or horror?' you ask. Together you select a movie starring a couple of actors you've both heard of and settle back into your seats, each covered with a blanket. Having your left ear connected to his right ear makes you feel like a giddy teenager, but not in a bad way.

You press 'play', the opening credits roll and you both almost levitate – you forgot to turn the sound down after testing your broken headphones. You press 'mute', and you both laugh as he adjusts the sound.

Watching the movie, you're acutely aware of the press of his leg and his arm against yours, sending little pin-pricks of desire through your body, and you struggle to focus on the film. It's almost too much having him touch you so innocuously, and you're tempted to casually shuffle an inch away from him, just to relieve your growing sense of sexual tension, but you can't bear to pull away from him. Every subtle shift in pressure has you analysing whether it's a tactical shift, or just him trying to get comfortable in the narrow airline seat.

Your thoughts briefly turn to Sven, waiting for you in Amsterdam, but you haven't even met him in person yet, and it's probably his fault you're turned on at the drop of a hat like this, after weeks of email foreplay.

About fifteen minutes into the movie, an explicit sex scene unfolds, and your mouth goes dry as you wonder if Ryan chose this movie deliberately. The man on the screen reaches for his lover, kissing her passionately. Then he tears open her blouse, revealing perfect breasts, the nipples taut and ridged around their edges. You can't drag your eyes away as the actor takes one in his mouth, lifting her skirt at the same time. Ryan squirms beside you, and the tent caused by his arousal under the blanket is very difficult to ignore. He catches you peeking and you both hastily look away.

As the actress takes off her partner's shirt, then

runs her nails down his chest, you slip a tentative hand under Ryan's blanket, running your fingertips hesitantly over his thigh. You hear him suck in a breath.

You both focus on the screen as the actor pulls off his lover's panties and buries his face between her legs.

Suddenly you feel his hand under your blanket, the touch of his fingers light as they trace your thigh, venturing under the hem of your skirt. You apply slightly more pressure on his leg by way of encouragement. His touch on your leg grows firmer and bolder, his fingers kneading, then climbing higher in slow incremental circles.

As the sex scene on screen hots up, you grow more brazen, closing your hand over his erection, which fills your palm underneath the blanket. His cock twitches, and unable to resist, you pull down his zip and run your hand along the length of his penis over the soft cotton of his underpants, then drop your hand down to cup his balls.

His own fingers travel even higher, and he begins to rub the outline of your pussy through your panties. Your knickers soak through at his touch and you push your mound up against his palm, parting your legs a little. Then you suck in your tummy as he tugs at the waistband of your knickers, his hand reaching inside the fabric, his skin warm on yours. He combs through your bush, then shifts to your slit, one finger running the length of it. The earplug falls from your ear as you writhe at his touch.

You both freeze as a flight attendant bustles past you down the darkened aisle, and you pull your hand away from his cock.

'I think I'll just go to the bathroom,' you whisper in his ear. 'You're welcome to join me.'

He reluctantly slides his finger out of you, teasing your clit for a few seconds before withdrawing his hand altogether.

You rearrange your skirt under the blanket, then get up and make your way through the darkened cabin, past the slumped and sleeping passengers, sensing him not far behind you.

You both cram into the cubicle and lock the door behind you. The space is so tiny, you're immediately jammed up against each other. Without saying a word, he grabs you, and for the first time his lips are on yours, his hot tongue in your mouth, his whole body pressed up against you.

Then his hands are busy with your blouse, fumbling to get your buttons open. He reaches for the clasp of your bra while pulling your skirt up to your waist, and you lunge for his cock, desperate to feel the silken hardness of it in your hands. You fumble with his button and zip, then yank down his pants, freeing his penis, which strains for the ceiling. Then his hands are in your knickers again, pulling them down your legs, and he makes contact with your pussy lips, teasing them with his fingers.

You gasp as a probing finger finds its way inside you once again. 'Do you want to fuck me?' you whisper in his ear, as your hand strokes his rock-like erection harder.

'Oh yes,' he groans.

'I want your cock inside me,' you whisper, not quite sure who you've turned into, but loving it nonetheless.

He turns you around, and you place both hands flat on the mirror in front of you, steaming it up with your breath. He bites at the back of your neck and your earlobe, then reaches around you and runs his hands down over your breasts. Stroking lower, he finds first your clit and then the opening of your pussy, and tests you with a finger again, the sound of your wetness against his fingertips audible. Then you hear the sound of a condom package being torn open, and that's your cue to spread your legs, lean forward and brace yourself.

One hand fondles your buttocks as the head of his penis nudges you from behind. You push your bottom up and back into him so that he can slip inside you, and you cry out as he stretches your pussy wide with his shaft, nudging his way further inside you, inch by inch, until he's in you all the way. 'Okay?' he mutters, and you respond, 'Oh God, yes.' He starts to fuck you, grunting with every stroke. It feels so good, you push back against his every thrust, at first in rhythm with him, and then later, when you're reaching the brink, wildly and out of control, the only sound your frantic breathing and skin slapping against skin.

'Don't stop,' you gasp, and seconds later, 'I'm coming,' and your entire body goes rigid as your muscles expand and contract, and for a moment you exist only in the middle of your orgasm, every sensation magnified. Then, with a few final slams, he comes too, squeezing both your arms with his hands, growling deep in his chest.

For several minutes, you both fight to regain your

breath. Then he whispers in your ear, 'Was it just me, or did we just experience some serious turbulence?'

You wait for your luggage at the carousel, a small smile on your face, the taste of Ryan – now racing to catch his connecting flight to Frankfurt – still on your lips. Your pocket vibrates and for a second you think it might be another aftershock from the series of orgasms you had. But it's just your phone – a text from your best friend, sent in response to your 'landed safely' message.

'Flight OK? What did you fly again?'

'Ryan Air' you text back. 'And it was un-fucking-believable.'

As your bag appears, you smile again: if the destination is half as good as the journey, you're in for a treat.

Go to page 57.

You've arrived in Amsterdam

Schiphol is more like an upmarket shopping mall than an airport. You wheel your suitcase past a clothing store, a luggage store, a coffee shop, a tourist trap selling 'I heart Amsterdam' t-shirts and bongs, and then slow down as you pass an upmarket sex shop.

It would be good to have a little nice-to-meet-you gift for Sven, you think, eyeing the little purple bullet-shaped device in the window. Is that what you think it is – one of those internal vibrators, complete with a tiny remote control? You dart into the shop, and spend your first euros in Amsterdam. Time will tell, you think, as you place the pretty pink package in your handbag and head for the fast train into the city, but you've got a feeling that it's money well spent.

Go to page 58.

You're on your way to meet the sculptor, good vibrations in your bag

You can hardly believe you're in Amsterdam at last. Butterflies run amok in your stomach as you make your way to the restaurant, smoothing down your dress, which is straight out of your suitcase and slightly crinkled. You've just dropped your luggage off at your hotel, and are en route to meet Sven in a quaint and artsy area called De Jordaan.

Here the streets are narrow and cobbled between canals. You pass houseboats, some with window boxes overflowing with bright flowers, others unused and unloved. Everything about this city is ancient, but somehow it never feels old, thanks to the people. In this area, they're an eclectic mix of young families, artists and tourists.

You pause at the edge of a canal to revisit the street map on your phone, beside the skeletal remains of a bicycle padlocked to the rails, only its spine remaining, the pedals and tyres long gone. You're finding Amsterdam easy to navigate – the train station is at the very apex and the streets and canals radiate outwards in logical rows. You double-check the location of De Tuin, the place where you're meeting him – you're almost there.

Suddenly racked with doubt, you check your reflection in a shop window. What if he doesn't show up? What if he does show up, but he looks nothing like the pictures he sent you? What if he's actually a pervert, a randy octogenarian or a scam artist eager to pilfer your bank account? You probably should have thought about all of this before you flew off to meet him. Anyway, it's too late to back out now. You've arrived at an unpretentious and cosy little bar-cum-restaurant with a deep-red awning. This is it ... you take a deep breath and step inside.

De Tuin is dimly lit, so you blink, then do a sweep of the room. You spot him almost immediately – thank goodness he resembles his profile pics – and your breath catches as your eyes meet. He smiles, gets to his feet and strides towards you. He's taller and more muscular than you were expecting from his pictures – you can make out his build beneath his simple long-sleeved t-shirt – and you take in olive skin, and the trace of a scar cutting through his left eyebrow. The cliché that chicks dig scars is a cliché for a reason, you think – it lends him a rugged allure. You wonder what caused it. A motorbike accident, perhaps – he seems the type – or maybe a dog bite? You have to curb the urge to trace it with your thumb.

'It's you . . .' he greets you in English, with a strong Dutch accent.

'And you . . .' you say. You smile at each other warmly. Then you put out a hand to shake his as he comes in for a hug. He draws back and then puts his hand out to shake yours as you lean forward for a hug. You both laugh.

'In Amsterdam we kiss hello like this,' he says, holding both your shoulders and kissing you on the cheek. He's tall and has to lean down to do it. You catch the scent of cologne with the bite of turpentine, the smell of an artist, the hands of an artist, too, rough and peppered with faint spatters of paint. And then he swoops in for a second kiss on your other cheek. Instinctively you pull back after the second kiss, thinking he's finished, but he tightens his grip and pulls you into him for a third kiss, back on the first cheek. 'Here, we kiss three times.'

You have to stop yourself from pointing to your lips and saying, 'Well, how many times do you kiss here?'

Sven guides you back to his table, and holds the chair out for you. Good-looking *and* chivalrous: he's really racking up the points.

You needn't have worried about making conversation: his spoken English is way better than his written English and, the occasional language hiccup aside, you find you have plenty to talk about, starting with the scar, which he got welding his first commission. But he says he's more experienced now, better with his hands these days. You wonder if the innuendo is deliberate.

All too soon you've ordered and eaten, simple but delicious food. Your plates are being cleared, and you look around to discover that you're the last two people in the café.

Sven puts his hand on your arm, letting it linger there for several seconds, and every nerve ending on your skin responds. 'We go back to my home for a nightcap?'

Why not? you think. It's not that late, and you didn't travel to Amsterdam to hang out in your hotel room.

You're impressed. Sven's loft is nestled between several upmarket apartment blocks overlooking a scenic canal.

The staircase leading up to it from the street is so steep and narrow, you have to go up in single file. You follow Sven, and can't help checking out his perfect backside the whole way up.

'Nice place,' you say, gazing at the interior, which, apart from the kitchen and a couple of doors that presumably lead to a bathroom and cupboards, is open-plan, with high ceilings and paint-splattered wooden floors. It's sparsely but stylishly furnished, the couch and table minimalist and chic, a modern four-poster bed against one wall. You're surprised at the lack of artwork on the walls.

'Would you like to drink something?' he asks.

'Please.'

He disappears into the kitchen and you take the opportunity to explore further, peering through a door that leads into a small, tidy bathroom, and another that connects to a studio space filled with art and sculptures.

Excited at the prospect of seeing his work, you step inside – and immediately regret it. Oh no. The first thing you see is a sculpture of a horribly disfigured man. His left eye bulges, his mouth is distended, and there's a hideous growth on the side of his head. You shiver and move on to the next piece: a landscape as seen by what can only be a deeply disturbed and chronically colour-blind person with absolutely no sense of humour. Your eye is drawn to another sculpture – a man and woman doubled over vomiting. Your stomach turns, and your nausea increases as you take in the other pieces displayed in the space: a photo-realistic painting of a dog taking a dump, and a garish oil of a leering clown that will be haunting your nightmares for months to come. You hear the whistle of the kettle arriving at the station, and quickly slip back into the loft, your head reeling.

You face the awful truth: Sven is possibly the worst artist you've ever come across. Why didn't you think of Googling his work before? His 'art' probably induces epilepsy or migraines. Worse, it makes a mockery of artists everywhere. It's truly, madly, deeply dire. Do you want to take things further with a guy who has such terrible taste?

If you decide to take things further, go to page 64.
If you decide to leave, go to page 74.

Sven reappears from the kitchen, and hands you a steaming mug. You sniff it: it smells unfamiliar, but is probably some kind of tea. You take a small sip, and scald your tongue. 'Shit!'

Sven takes the cup from you and puts it down besides his.

'I kiss better,' he says, and before you can respond, he hooks a finger in the pocket of your dress, looks into your eyes for a long moment, then leans in and presses his mouth on yours. His lips are soft and warm – this is better than cyber-sex any day – and you instantly forget your seared tongue.

One hand unzips your dress as the other strokes the bare skin of your neck, then slips down your back, tracing the path revealed as your zip peels open. He keeps kissing you, his skilled tongue exploring your mouth as his fingers trail up and down your spine, unravelling you.

'God, you're beautiful. I want to paint you,' he murmurs.

'I've never had my portrait painted before,' you say, slightly concerned – you're not sure you're

64

ready for a hall-of-weird-mirrors version of your-self.

'No, I don't want to paint you . . .' he says.

'I think whatever compliment you're trying to pay me has been lost in translation.'

He looks at you, clearly confused. 'I am saying I want to paint *on* you.'

'On me?'

'Your skin is more beautiful than canvas.'

Ah, suave. How many women have fallen for this line? But you're a little relieved, to be honest; at least you won't have to see his painting if it's on you – and his offer is certainly intriguing.

He steps back from you, and pulls his shirt off to reveal a tight white vest, his muscles rippling under-neath the fabric. Then, all business, he disappears into the adjoining studio and emerges moments later with a palette, brushes and some tubes of paint. 'Acrylics,' he explains. 'Don't worry, they wash off.'

He drops the painting paraphernalia on the bedside table, then he takes you by the shoulders and spins you around. With your exposed back to him, he sweeps your hair away from the nape of your neck, kissing the delicate, sensitive skin there before trailing his mouth to your earlobe, making goosebumps rise. Slowly he pulls your dress down over your shoulders and it slithers to the floor, leaving you in nothing but bra, panties and heels. Then he turns you back around and kiss-steps you backwards until the bed presses against your legs and you both collapse on to it.

You keep kissing and caressing each other, learning each other's mouths and fingertips, and then he straddles you on the bed, and reaches for his palette. Fascinated, you watch as he squeezes lumps of colour on to it, yellow, blue, red and white. He mixes a little blue and yellow paint with his finger and it swirls into a perfect deep green. Then he returns his attention to you, the paint-smeared finger poised above you.

'Wait, you're going to get paint on your sheets,' you say.

'Fuck the sheets!' he growls, bringing his finger down to the dip below your neck where your collarbones meet, drawing a long line down the middle of your torso, stopping only when he reaches the delicate edging of your panties. Then he drops the palette on the bed beside your head, and unclips the front fastening of your bra, pulling it away on either side to expose your breasts. You're suddenly embarrassed by the intensity of his artist's gaze, so you cover yourself with your arms. He reaches for your wrists and drops down on to you, devouring you with his mouth, literally disarming you. You giggle as you notice that he now has a green stripe, transferred from your chest, running down the middle of his vest.

He pulls his vest off over his head in one movement, and you're not disappointed. His skin is tanned, and he has a dusting of light-blond hairs on his chest. He's muscular, but not in a gym kind of way – rather in a blow-torch, box-lugging, canvas-stretching, welding kind of way. Which is perfect, you think.

He returns to his palette and this time he dips his finger into the red paint. With great concentration, he traces a wide circle around the outside of your left breast, his breath warm on your skin. Then, his finger never leaving your body, he crosses over the green meridian he created earlier. Satisfied, he briefly replenishes the paint on his finger and repeats the process for your other breast. You're pleased to feel his erection tight against you as he straddles you, and you press up against him, your pussy wet and aching, yearning for even the tiniest bit of friction.

Next, Sven dips his finger into the yellow paint and

draws another circle, this time much closer to your nipple, but still not actually touching it. He scoops up more paint and heads over to your other nipple, but instead of circling it, he draws a line bisecting your breast, starting at the top and tracing his way down. He slows as he tracks over the nipple itself, which is puckered with excitement, and a moan escapes your lips. It's almost too much to take, the intensity of his focus, the swoosh of his finger over your body, but you're hungry for more. You try to sit up and nuzzle at his neck, but he pushes you back down gently, still intent on his art.

This time, when he reaches for the palette, he mixes green and yellow together and traces a spiral on your belly until he reaches the top of your panties. He draws a line along the tender skin of your bikini line, and you groan as he moves on to your legs, painting long stripes down one, and ripples down the other, starting at your inner thigh, eventually making his way down to your ankles, then back up to your thighs again.

And then at last, with a generous dollop of purple finger-mixed from blue and red, he paints over your panties, first in rows perpendicular to your slit, and then at last in one long line that starts at your belly button and drops down over your mound, and follows the line of your pussy lips down between your legs, and all the way round and under to your bottom. You squirm, desperate for him to do it again. And he does, but even slower.

'Enough art,' you breathe, rolling him over on to his back so you're straddling him, and this time he doesn't fight you. You look down at his face and stroke your thumb over the scar slicing through his eyebrow, something you've been wanting to do since the first moment you saw him; then you drop your body down on to him and press your chest against his, transferring the paint from your chest on to his, slipping and sliding down his body. You kiss, twisting and turning so that you're pressing your hungry pussy against the bulge in his pants, then tug open the buttons of his Levi's and lift yourself as he pulls off his underpants and jeans all in one movement.

Then he stretches past you into the drawer of his bedside table, pulling out a condom and ripping the packaging open. You take it from him, scoot back down his body, and roll it on over his pulsing, paint-covered cock. Then you crawl back up the length of his body and hover above him for a moment or two, before dropping down on him, his cock pushing deep up into you, making you cry out and bite down on his shoulder, causing him to buck up into you even harder.

Then everything is just a swirl of paint and colour as you fuck hard and fast. He comes before you, with a shout, but you keep on pumping, controlling the speed and intensity of your contact – you know what to do to reach your own orgasm, which is close. With his slowly softening cock still inside you, you keep grinding, with just the right amount of friction against your clit, until you come with a shudder, the taste of paint on the scalded tip of your tongue.

You lie together in a tangle of smeared sheets, sweat and paint caking and drying on your bodies in the night air.

'I can't wait to show you my art and my city,' Sven says.

You mumble something into the pillow, and nod off to sleep, curled inside his body like a comma.

You wake up several hours later, momentarily wondering where you are. Then you feel the stiffness of paint on your skin, and remember. You lie still next to Sven, whose breathing reveals that he's lost in sleep. Even though it was a fun night, the conversation was a little stilted, but you can't blame the guy – you wouldn't be a great raconteur in a second or third language either. There's no denying the sex was incredibly hot. But then there was his hideous art. Godawful is the only appropriate way to describe it. You're really surprised: you had expected eclectic, maybe rough and rugged – a bit like him – but not the monstrosities you saw. There's no way you'll to be able to hide the look of horror on your face when he shows it to you later. Artists can be very sensitive, and you doubt he'll take it well if you tell him that his work, particularly the vomiting stuff, is a self-fulfilling prophecy.

You inch away from him and creep out of bed, paint cracking and flaking off your body. You freeze as he grunts and turns, a streak of paint dark across his chin, mimicking the scar through his eyebrow, then you tiptoe away, grabbing your clothes and pulling them on as you go, hurrying barefoot and paint-covered out of the apartment and into the Amsterdam dawn. You pull on your heels and walk along the edge of the canal, breathing in the fresh early-morning air, trying to work out if you're going in the right direction to get back to your hotel.

Fortunately, Sven doesn't know where you're staying. You hunt around in your handbag until you find the bit of paper on which you wrote his phone number and address. Then, as you approach a bridge, you drop it, letting it flutter leaf-like into the water. You hurry across the bridge – only just avoiding being run down by a bicycle in the process – and watch the paper float out the other side, before being swallowed by the canal's black depths. Watching his contact details disappear, you feel slightly guilty for running out on him like that – after all, he has no idea you've seen his horrendous life's work. You tell yourself you'll message him a little later, thanking him for the night, making up some excuse, and apologising for leaving so abruptly and permanently.

You lean against the wall of the bridge, looking at the water as the sky turns purple and lightens. It's not all bad. You've had fun, and so what if you didn't find exactly what you were looking for? You've got twenty-four hours left in one of the most fascinating cities in the world. There are museums, shops and restaurants galore to explore.

A thought strikes you. Once your time in Amsterdam is up, there's no reason why you couldn't extend your adventure. Why not see if Firefly in New York is still keen to meet? And then there's your mysterious Count in Venice ...

To zoot off to Italy and carouse with the Count, go to page 113.
To contact Firefly and wing your way to the city that never sleeps, go to page 245.

73

You've decided to leave Sven's apartment

Sven appears from the kitchen, carrying two steaming cups. He hands you your tea, and you cradle it between your palms, blowing on it. It's far too hot to sip – you don't want to burn your tongue.

'Dinner was great – thank you,' you say.

'It was a pleasure,' he says. 'I enjoyed it also.'

You mock-yawn and look at your watch. 'Actually, I'm shattered. It must be all the travel. I think I'm going to head back to my hotel and get some rest.'

You can't help noticing that Sven looks a little disappointed. 'Maybe I can show you around tomorrow?' he offers. 'It's a great time of year to be in Amsterdam. I could show you some of my work, then we could go to a museum, get some lunch ...'

Your heart plummets when he mentions his work. You're not sure if you're a good enough actor to pretend to like it.

'That sounds nice,' you manage.

'Taxi?' he asks, and you nod gratefully. He reaches for his phone, and ten minutes later a hoot sounds from outside. Sven walks you to the door, and as you turn to thank him once more, he draws you to him, taking you by surprise. His lips are soft and warm, his kiss searching and hungry, and you're aware of his stubble pricking your chin. You respond to his tongue, which is hot and probing. All too soon, the taxi hoots again, and he pulls away from you.

'Tomorrow we will see some things,' he says.

You make your way down the narrow stairs on jelly legs, Sven close behind you. As the taxi pulls away, you look back and see him standing in the doorway, haloed by the light from inside. Unexpected desire ripples through you, and you wonder if you haven't made a bad judgement call. Thank goodness there's still tomorrow night, which suddenly feels very far away.

You've arranged to meet Sven at his studio, a few streets from his apartment. On the way, you amble through the Noordermarkt, a small farmers' market set up in a triangular space beside a canal. It's a cornucopia of fresh organic food, and the perfect breakfast spot. You stop for strong, fragrant coffee and crêpes, with late blackberries, soured cream and brown sugar – after all, you need fortifying for the day's adventures ahead. Feeling much stronger, you locate the studio and press the buzzer, bracing yourself.

'At last, you get to see my studio and my work,' Sven says, taking your hand and leading you through the door. Gut filled with dread, you steel yourself to look at more hideous art: you've been practising your fake 'oh-I-love-it' face in the mirror at your hotel.

As you walk into his studio, the first thing you see is a large bronze sculpture of a man and a woman embracing, and your breath catches in your throat. This is not what you were expecting.

'Can I touch it?' you whisper.

Sven nods.

You run your fingers gently over the woman's slightly lifted skirt. The folds of her dress look so soft and real, as if caught in a draught. It's hard to believe you're touching immovable metal, and not silk. And while cold to the touch, there's something incredibly warm about the sculpture, as if the couple's passion is heating it from within. You don't have to fake anything; your 'oh-I-love-it' face is all natural.

You move along to the next piece, a charcoal drawing of a horse. The sinews of its flanks are drawn with such skill and sensitivity, you expect it to gallop off the wall. You glance around the studio and take in half-a-dozen more pieces, some hanging, some stacked against the walls, each one more passionately crafted than the last. You can't see a piece in the room that you wouldn't want to own.

'They're incredible,' you say at last, your voice only just audible.

'You are surprised?' he asks.

'I'm not, well, I am … it's just … this isn't at all like your other stuff.'

'What other stuff?'

'The work back at your place.'

'What work? Are you meaning in the room next to my loft?'

You nod tentatively.

'That's not my work!'

'It's not?'

'No! You think I would make that? People vomiting?' He takes a step back, horrified. 'That belongs to a friend of mine. He's having some life problems, treatment for drugs, he lost his kids in his divorce. I'm keeping his work until he is managing better.'

You squirm. How could you have thought that hideous stuff was his? The man you've been chatting to online could never have created those ghastly pieces.

'I knew they couldn't possibly be yours,' you say, trying to back-pedal. 'Your work is like you: beautiful, creative and incredibly sensuous.'

You see his jaw loosen and inwardly mop your brow. That could have gone very wrong, very fast.

'So. The city,' you say, changing the subject. 'What shall we see first?'

'That depends. What side of Amsterdam do you want to see?' he asks.

'What sides are there?'

'Well, you don't have a lot of time, and Amsterdam has many sides, so you must decide. We can do the more cultural side of Amsterdam, or the sexier side. Your choice.'

If you want to see the cultural side of Amsterdam, go to page 79.

If you want to see the sexier side of Amsterdam, go to page 102.

78

You're going to see the cultural side of Amsterdam

You've seen footage of Amsterdam's red-light district, and that's not really your bag.

'Let's get cultural,' you say. 'What do you have in mind?'

Sven thinks for a moment. 'What about the Van Gogh Museum? A lot of tourists go there, but it is one of my favourite places in Amsterdam.'

You suddenly recall the small purple bullet vibrator in your bag. A museum would be a perfect setting for a test drive. 'I like the sound of that,' you say, and Sven's face lights up like a Christmas tree, your earlier *faux pas* clearly forgiven and forgotten.

There's only one small decision you still have to make: who gets to be in control during this little excursion? Do you keep the remote control to yourself and secretly take matters into your own hands? Or do you share your toys, and give up full control to Sven?

On the one hand, it would be incredibly decadent to give yourself a discreet orgasm in a public space – and a very famous museum, no less – without anyone knowing what you're up to. On the other hand, wouldn't it be fun to have a partner in crime?

If you want to give Sven the remote control, go to page 81.

If you want to keep the remote control for yourself, go to page 90.

You've decided to give Sven the remote control

You head into the studio bathroom and examine your face in the mirror. Who is this crazy woman taking what she wants from life? It feels like you hardly know her, but you like her.

What the hell, you think. You're far from home, and highly unlikely to bump into anyone you know. Even if this all goes pear-shaped, you don't ever have to see Sven again after tomorrow, so what do you have to lose?

You sit on the toilet seat, open the packaging and take out the purple device – something between a large bullet and a small slightly elongated egg, with a string at one end. The accompanying remote control looks like a garage door opener with three buttons: a power button, a button with a plus sign, and another with a minus sign on it.

You turn on the power and the bullet vibrates in your palm. You click the plus sign and take the device through all five of its settings, ranging from a gentle buzz all the way up to the highest setting, which sets it off into a blur of vibrations in your hand.

You turn it off, and, hands shaking, you unbutton

your jeans, slip down your panties, and carefully insert the bullet. You only feel the very slightest pressure inside you when you stand up.

Then you place the remote control back into the box, wrap the whole thing in several tissues and tie it up with a pink hair-band you find in the detritus at the bottom of your bag. You button your jeans, wash your hands, compose yourself, then nod at your reflection in the mirror before stepping back into the studio.

'I brought you something,' you say, holding out the small box in its makeshift wrapping.

Sven looks up, surprised, but pleasantly so. 'For me?'

'It's sort of for both of us,' you say.

He tears into the wrapping, dropping it on the floor. You can't help smiling; you read somewhere that you can tell a lot about what kind of lover someone is by the way they open a gift. There are the 'slow pickers', who peel everything off carefully so as not to damage any of it, perhaps intending to reuse the paper later; and then there are the 'wanton tearers', so eager to get into the package that they barely spare a thought for the wrapping. They're the ones that rip your clothes

off to get to you. It seems like you've found yourself
a wanton tearer.

Sven holds the remote control in his calloused hand,
looking at it curiously.

'What is it?' he asks, turning it over.

'A remote control.'

'Controlling what?'

You pick the discarded box up off the floor and
show him the photograph of the purple bullet on the
box.

It takes Sven a minute to figure out what it is, and
then a small smile creeps across his face. He considers
the remote, turning it over in his palm. 'But where is
it?'

You swallow hard and point at your lap – your
pussy tingling at your own boldness – and his jaw
drops.

'Haven't we got a museum to visit?' you say, grabbing your bag and coat and bolting for the door,
unable to hold his gaze for another second.

Sven catches up with you, takes your hand and
leads you through the streets. Canals, people and bicycles everywhere, the scent of baking, hot oil, coffee
and sometimes a whiff of reefer as you pass cafés, the

earthy smell of fallen leaves and moped fumes. You have to keep your wits about you – you've been in Amsterdam for less than twenty-four hours, and you've almost stepped into the path of oncoming bicycles at least four times and a tram once.

Sven points to a tram heading in your direction, and you have to dash the last few yards to catch it. He pays for you, then follows you down the aisle. As the tram pulls away, you lose your balance and stumble back against him, feeling the heft of his body, his chest hard and strong against your back. You take a seat, and he slides into one behind but across the aisle from you. You can sense his eyes boring into the back of your neck.

The tram turns sharply on its rails and you grab on to the seat in front of you. Then, you jump as a slight vibration starts in your pussy. You whip your head around to Sven, who's leaning back casually in his seat, looking out of the window, whistling innocently.

You face forward again, focusing on the sensation. It's a minor tremor, almost imperceptible over and above the existing vibrations of the tram, but it's definitely there. Suddenly it ramps up a notch, and you whirl in your seat again. Sven is still gazing out of the window, but his eyes are crinkled with mischief.

Determined not to let him see you responding further, you close your eyes as the device ratchets up one more notch. The pulsations in your pussy are sublime, and you have to clench your thighs together and concentrate hard to keep your feelings from showing on your face. You clutch the seat in front of you, squeezing it so tightly that your knuckles turn white.

The vibrations stop. You clear your throat, open your eyes, and sit up straight, unclenching your fingers from the seat. You won't give Sven the satisfaction of making eye contact again, you think, crossing your legs nonchalantly and acting as if nothing has happened. You stay on full alert for any further movement down under, but the bullet remains quiet, and you're grateful for the opportunity to regain your composure and take in some of the sights and sounds of Amsterdam. It's like no other city you've ever visited – heavy with the weight of centuries, dark stone and brick, but made vibrant by the colour, brush and hurry of the people who live in it. Eventually you turn and smile at Sven, and the bulge in his lap is impossible to miss.

Good, you think, at least you're not the only one who's impossibly turned on.

Together you join the queue of tourists at the entrance to the Van Gogh Museum, and you're momentarily distracted from your interesting internal situation by the unusual architecture. You're surprised at how starkly modern the building is, a cluster of glass and concrete boxes.

'Are you all right?' Sven murmurs in your ear.

'Never better,' you say with a small smile. 'But maybe we need to lay down some ground rules.'

'I have no problem with rules.'

'I think we need a sign to tell you when to stop and when to go.'

Sven thinks for a moment. 'How about the art?' he suggests. 'If you say you like a piece of art, that means "go", and if you say you don't like something, that means "stop".'

You nod, and Sven slings an arm around you, kissing you hard. His left leg slides between yours, and you're hyper-aware of the pressure of his thigh against the crotch of your jeans, the bullet an unmoving but solid presence inside you. The knowledge that Sven has control of it is a tantalising secret. You kiss him more deeply, forgetting for a moment that there's a crowd of culture-hungry tourists around you.

'Let's go see some art,' Sven says, smiling down at you.

And so you wander through the museum on high alert, waiting for him to turn on the bullet. Passionate about the work, Sven stops to consider every piece, sharing titbits of information about Van Gogh in his Dutch-accented English – it's like having your own personal (and very hot) tour guide. After a while, you wonder if he's forgotten about the remote in his pocket and the bullet lodged inside you, and you decide to do the same and just enjoy the art. Half an hour later, you're completely absorbed in *The Yellow House* when there's a sudden tremor inside you. Sven is standing next to you, innocently studying the next painting along, his hands in his pockets.

You steady yourself, planting your legs a little wider, and concentrate on keeping your breathing even. He sidles up to you. 'What do you think of this one?' he asks.

You swallow hard. 'This one?' you say, trying to keep your voice even. 'I like it.' Then you walk slowly on, stopping in front of the next painting, a study of a tree in blossom. As you pause, the vibrations inside you crank up a notch, and it takes all your willpower to keep a straight face.

Sven sidles over to you, and drops his hand on to the base of your spine, applying just the slightest pressure. 'What about this one?' he asks, his voice hoarse.

'I quite like this one, too, but it's not my favourite yet,' you say, sucking your bottom lip, and pretending to examine the piece. But your heart is starting to race, the vibrations are thrumming through your g-spot, and you feel the slow build of an orgasm starting.

Sven takes your hand and, with the bullet still pulsating, he leads you to the next painting, then ramps up the power one more notch. There's no longer anything subtle about it and, not trusting your knees to hold you upright, you find a bench and sit, crossing your legs tightly. Sven settles beside you, holding your body against his, as your orgasm begins its slow burn from deep inside you. There's very little you can do once it gets started, so you let it tear through you in waves until you can't stand the vibrations any more.

'I don't like this one,' you shout out, still in the throes of coming. 'I don't like this one at all!'

Gradually, the vibrations slow, and the last of the orgasm trembles through your body. You look up and it dawns on you that you've been yelling that you don't like one of Van Gogh's most famous self-portraits. A serious-looking couple who probably have four degrees in Art History between them shoot you horrified looks, and Van Gogh himself peers sadly at you from behind his easel.

You drop your head into Sven's shoulder, and take in the musky smell of him, noticing that his cock is pulsing under the fabric of his jeans, straining at the zip. It seems he's sharing your excitement.

'You really don't like it? I don't know ...' Sven says, squeezing your hand in his. 'This might just be my new most favourite painting.'

THE END

You've decided to keep the remote control for yourself

The Van Gogh Museum is magnificent. From the outside, it's almost brutally modern, the glass, steel and concrete piled up like children's blocks. Inside, it's a haven, even with the crowds thronging through. You always find it moving when you see famous works of art for the first time – they're often smaller, or bigger, or more textured, the colours richer or more subtle than you imagined.

The two of you stroll through the rooms together, Sven answering your questions about the artwork. It's clear he knows the place like the back of his hand.

After a while, you excuse yourself and find the nearest bathroom. In the privacy of a cubicle, you remove the bullet from its packaging, read the instructions, and, taking a deep breath, insert it inside you.

Next, you stand, adjust your clothing, and turn the remote control to its lowest setting, bracing yourself for the experience. The bullet buzzes to life inside of you, making you start. It's a strange sensation – you've never vibrated from the inside before. Tentatively, you take a step or two in your cubicle and find that

90

moving is comfortable, so you turn it up a notch, then up one more to test its power. Not wanting to get yourself too aroused quite yet, you turn it off.

You shiver with anticipation as you wash your hands. It's a huge turn-on that Sven will never know that you're coming while you're Goghing.

Back in the museum, you find him studying the famous painting of purple irises. He's so focused, he barely notices you. Standing next to him, you slip your hand into your pocket and turn the remote to its lowest setting, feeling the bullet buzz to life inside you. It's not enough to get you over-excited, but you're aware of it as a subtle thrum.

Sven takes your hand as you walk to the next painting, the only sign that he knows you're even there. You're not bothered – it's kind of cute how passionate he is about artworks he's seen so many times before.

Surreptitiously, you turn the remote up a notch, and can't help squeezing Sven's hand as the bullet doubles its speed. It's not so subtle now, and the inner walls of your pussy hum with the vibrations. You discover that if you squeeze your pussy muscles, it makes your clit vibrate too, causing the most sensational feeling – one you know could make you come

91

in minutes. But that would be too soon; you want to draw this out a little.

In the next room, you spot a bench and make your way over to it, pretending to admire the art in front of you, while Sven concentrates on one of Van Gogh's self-portraits. You turn the remote to its highest setting, and lean back on your arms as the bullet goes ballistic inside you. Slowly you clench and unclench your pussy muscles, making the vibrations alter in intensity as they radiate up your spine. Now that you're sitting, you can even feel them in your buttocks – your entire lower body is buzzing.

You can't hold on any longer – your orgasm rounds the corner and barrels towards you. You cross your legs tightly, intensifying the buzzing even more, and close your eyes, your heart pounding in your ears. You can't suppress your moan as you come powerfully, then scramble to turn off the remote in your pocket so you can focus on looking as inconspicuous as possible while catching your breath.

You open your eyes and glance around, the room gradually coming back into focus. Fortunately, only a bored-looking security guard in the far corner of the room and an elderly woman are staring at you.

Sven is examining a sculpture intently, and you stand up carefully and walk over to him on baby-deer legs.

'It's beautiful,' you say, examining the bronze bust of a woman.

'I want to make you,' he says, making you shiver as his lips drift past your ear.

'You mean you want to do me?'

'That also,' he says with a sheepish look. 'But I mean I want to make you – you know, a bust of you. I could make something better than this!'

'You think so?' you say, your aching post-orgasm pussy contracting again at the thought of his hands finally touching you.

'So, how exactly does this work?' you ask.

'It is simple. You take your clothes off and I make a mould of your body with the plaster of Paris. And then I bronze that.' You're back at his loft, *sans* bullet. Sven is already elbow-deep in a bucket of white paste, stirring it up. Technically you've already had an orgasm in front of this guy – and Van Gogh, too – so being naked in front of him doesn't seem like such a big deal.

In the bathroom, you remove your jeans and the bullet, aware that your pussy has woken up again. You're amazed (and secretly rather pleased) by your appetite for sex. Sven has barely touched you – your earlier orgasm was pretty much all your own doing – so you're looking forward to him paying a little attention to your body. Leaving only your knickers on, you wrap a large white bath towel around yourself and head back out into the loft.

Sven has turned on some music, smearing white paste across his iPod in the process. A painter's drop-cloth has been spread over the floor in the middle of the room. You hover at the bathroom door, and he summons you over with instructions to step on to the cloth, all business.

You obey, clutching the towel with one hand, wondering what you've got yourself into.

Sven tries to blow his curly fringe off his face, and when it won't budge, he swipes at it with a finger, leaving a white smudge across his forehead. You smile at how silly he looks, a deathly serious expression on a face smeared with white gunk, and it releases some of your tension.

'What happens next?' you ask.

Sven reaches for a sheet of muslin and begins to tear it into strips, the muscles in his arms rippling with the effort, and any doubts you were having melt away at the thought of having those capable hands all over you.

'Cover yourself in this first,' Sven says, holding out a large jar of Vaseline. 'That way the plaster doesn't stick.'

You turn your back to him, spread your legs slightly, and drop your towel to the ground.

'Can you do my back for me? I don't want to miss a spot,' you say. The room is silent, except for the thud of your heart in your chest, which you hope only you can hear. Sven steps close to you, his breath warm on your shoulders.

'This can be cold,' he says, his mouth close to your ear. You shut your eyes, loving the curl of his accent. Then his hands are on you, smearing the cool Vaseline on to your skin, his hands strong, but still delicate even through the brush of callouses and scars.

'Finished,' he says at last.

You pivot slowly, turning to face him. 'Not quite,' you say.

Sven dips his hand into the Vaseline, and there's no

mistaking the need darkening his eyes as he wipes a stripe across the top of your chest, then another down the middle, tracking between your breasts. Then he covers your stomach with the jelly, and eventually slathers it over each of your breasts, his palm gently swiping down over your nipples.

Once he has you covered, he reaches for the first piece of muslin, dips it into the paste and covers your front in a criss-cross fashion, smoothing each piece of fabric down with the heel of his hand. You raise your arms so he can reach your sides. He has to work quickly, so that the plaster doesn't set before he's finished. Once he's covered your front, he moves behind you, and makes a second cast of your back.

The plaster begins to warm and harden on your skin. You notice a sheen of perspiration on Sven's brow, and he pulls his shirt off over his head. The fuzz of blond hair over skin as smooth as his own bronzes is irresistible – if you could move, you would be unable to stop yourself reaching out to stroke his chest. The sexual tension reverberates between you as he runs his fingers over the stiffening muslin.

'There,' he says, stepping back from you when

you're completely covered in plaster-smeared muslin, front and back.

He clears up and washes his hands while the cast sets, pulling and tightening against your skin. When he's satisfied that it's set, he carefully pulls the cast from the front of your body, then the one from your back, laying both pieces on the drop cloth to dry further. You feel naked after the protection of the cast, so you cover your breasts with your arms.

'Now what?' you ask, your voice just a whisper. You're desperate for him to touch you not because he wants to make art out of you, or because he wants to save you from stepping into the path of a speeding bicycle, but purely because he wants to.

'You can shower if you want?' Sven says tentatively.

'You've got a little . . .' you say, touching the smear of plaster on his forehead.

'Maybe I'd better join you then,' he says.

'Maybe.'

And at that, Sven sweeps you up, kissing you with a day's worth of pent-up passion. He carries you into the bathroom, and you giggle as he almost loses his balance. He puts you down briefly to unbuckle and unzip his plaster-spattered jeans, and you strip off your panties and step into the shower. Sven follows, almost tripping on his jeans in his desperation to get them off.

As the hot water cascades down your bodies, you lather up a sponge and begin to rub off the remnants of Vaseline and plaster. He takes it from you and wipes you in long strokes, starting at the top of your chest and working his way down. You tilt your head back, enjoying the feeling of the sponge, rough as a cat's tongue on your skin.

When he's finished washing your front and your back, you turn, capture the sponge and take over, wiping down his chest and arms, then his legs and finally his thighs. Then you start to sponge his groin, starting with his balls and working your way up his cock, squeezing its hardness with your free hand as he leans back against the shower wall, groaning as you run both your hand and the sponge up and down.

Dropping to your haunches, you take his penis into your mouth and suck powerfully, while continuing to rub and clasp the shaft, your hand twisting around its thickness. And then Sven pulls you up to him, saying something in Dutch before cupping your chin in his hand. He lifts you again, and you wrap your legs around him as he turns off the taps and carries you out of the shower, setting you down on the sink counter. The room is so filled with steam that he looks fuzzy at the edges – but he's definitely real, hard flesh-and-blood.

You attack his neck with your mouth, nibbling and nipping as he feels one-handed for something in the cabinet. Then you're urging him on as he tears at the wrapping of a condom, and you help him slide the ribbed latex on to his pulsing cock. You spread your legs, as he nudges the tip against your slit till he finds the entrance to your pussy. At last he slides inside you, and after the teasing and solo shenanigans of the entire day, having him stretch you and then fill you up to the hilt is pure delight.

You half-growl, half-purr as he fucks you, alternating the depths of every thrust, so you don't know what's coming next, whether he's going to ram into you all the way, or tease you with a slow, shallow press. You can tell he's holding back because he wants to enjoy the experience, make it last.

But you want to, need to come now, so you rock your hips forward to urge him into a rhythm, and he starts to pound into you almost to the beat of a track.

Clutching at him, tugging his hair, all the muscles in his back tensing under your fingertips, you breathe 'Wait' into his ear, feeling your orgasm approaching and there's a second where you're terrified he'll stop doing exactly what he's doing. But then he slides his thumb on to your clit, and you come so hard the room spins.

You throw your head back against the bathroom mirror, your pussy contracting around Sven's solid cock, which is still pumping inside you, your calves pressed against his tight, perfect bum.

His head drops back and it's his turn to grunt out an orgasm, the cords in his neck flexing as he shouts out something in Dutch – it must be their version of *oh God, oh God, oh God*, or maybe it's *oh fuck, oh fuck, oh fuck* – either way, it's a huge release of tension, as his entire body spasms again and again. Then the weight of his body slumps against yours, his head dropping into the crook of your neck, his cock still pulsing inside you. You unlock your ankles from around his back, and lean against the mirror, both of you still breathing heavily.

You might just have to extend your trip, you think with a smile, as you trail your fingers up his back, feeling the ridges and dips of his spine. After all, there's still so much of Amsterdam to explore. More importantly, you should probably stick around and see how your bust turns out.

THE END

You want to see the sexier side of Amsterdam

'So, you definitely want to see the sexier side of Amsterdam?' Sven says.

'When in Rome ...' you say. 'What about a live sex show? I've heard those are wild!'

'Are you sure?' he asks.

'Why not? Surely you don't get a sexier side of Amsterdam than that.'

'If you say so,' he says. 'Last chance? We could always go to a museum, or something like that instead.'

If you'd rather go to a museum than a live sex show, go to page 79.

If you want to go to a live sex show, go to page 103.

You've chosen to see a live sex show

Minutes after you take your seats, a couple walk out on to the stage, holding hands. The male performer is slightly shorter than his partner, his body well-built and muscular. She's tall and rangy, wearing a skirt, blouse and high heels, an outfit that could be the uniform of a legal secretary or a school teacher, but somehow it manages to look suggestive.

The couple make their way to the circular bed on the stage, the lights dim and the music lifts, and the man starts to kiss the woman on the side of the mouth. He makes quick, practised work of her clothes, without so much as a natural hitch at the clasp of her bra, or a fumble at his own belt buckle, and within seconds both of them are completely naked. It all happens so quickly it's as if their clothes have simply melted off, and then they're having sex, just like that. You're not sure why you're so surprised – it's not like you were expecting him to take her out for dinner and a movie first – but it's just all so sudden. And so unsexy.

You'd thought it would be erotic to watch, but there's something really clinical about it. A drunken stag-party crew in the third row begin to whoop and cheer, and you feel vaguely nauseated.

The couple on stage start out in the missionary position and every few minutes, they transition smoothly into a new contortion, like a scheduled and coordinated dance routine, with none of the passion and hunger you'd imagined you'd see. As the guy flips his partner over to take her doggy-style, and the bed rotates away from you, you can't help stifling a yawn. Sven notices, and you pull a face at him.

'Come on,' he says, pulling you out of the theatre and past a man in a trench coat hunched in the back. You avert your eyes – that's certainly not what you paid to see.

You stand together in the street a couple of feet away from the entrance to the club, and watch the comings and goings around you – literally. The cobbled side street is lined with windows, and a range of women in every kind of lingerie pose in the windows, trying to attract passers-by. A man nips through the door beside a window that frames a particularly busty woman, and she immediately closes her curtain so she can welcome him in private. Five minutes later, he'll leave somewhat lighter, literally and fiscally. It's a fascinating exchange, but a business one – it's about as mechanical and unsensual as the show you've just seen.

'I'm sorry,' you say, 'that was awful. It wasn't anything like I thought it would be.'

'What were you expecting?' he asks.

'I thought it would be sexy, or something, but that wasn't the least bit sensuous. It was like watching robots. I suppose some fantasies are best left to the imagination.'

'What would you like to do next?' he asks, taking your hands.

'I don't know. What's one of your fantasies? How about we do that?'

He looks into your eyes. 'You want for sure?'

You square your shoulders. 'Why not? How wild could it be?'

He stares at you, then starts to smile. 'Okaaay,' he says. 'How about this … ?'

If his fantasy is a little wild, go to page 106.
If his fantasy is a little surprising, go to page 112.

His fantasy is a little wild

The silk scarf tightens around your wrists as Sven ties first one arm to the bedpost, and then the other. You can't see anything with the blindfold over your eyes, but that seems to make all your other senses more acute. He withdraws for a moment, and then you feel the warmth of his hand on your ankle, silk against your skin again, and the tug of the binding being tied to the bottom of the bed. There's a brief flicker of alarm as he ties your other leg to the end of the bed, and you realise you're entirely at his mercy.

But then his mouth is on yours, hard and passionate. He wraps his tongue around yours, lashing at it, driving out your anxiety, and even though you haven't known him very long, you realise two things: you trust this man; and you want him to fuck you.

He roams your mouth, neck and the edge of your ear, taking the tender lobe between his teeth, then flicking it with the flat of his tongue. You want to stroke him, run your fingers through his hair, but there's nothing you can do with your arms and legs tied like this, other than kiss him back, bite, nibble, suck whenever any part of him comes near your mouth. You're acutely aware of the taste and smell of him – hot, salty, musky with that now-familiar tang of turpentine.

His mouth travels from your ear to the soft underside of your jaw, and then down your chest as your heart speeds. Then he moves back to kiss you, and you can feel his fingers unbuttoning your blouse and pulling it open. Then he shifts away from you, breaking contact, and you sense him gazing at you as you wriggle underneath him.

Once again, his fingers explore, lower this time, stroking your belly, then scraping over your mound and down. 'Your panties are so wet,' he growls, and you gasp as he eases them down your thighs. There's a ripping sound as he tears the delicate fabric free of your legs, and you hear them swish to the floor. Then you hear the metallic sounds of a belt buckle and a zip, and more soft thuds as his clothes get tossed on to the floor.

You feel the weight of his body on you once again, as he straddles your body and then his rock-solid cock settles along the length of your soaking cunt.

'What do you want?' he murmurs, his voice surprisingly close to your ear; you thought he was sitting upright, but he's obviously leaning low over you.

'I want you to fuck me,' you whisper faintly.

'What you say? I can't hear you!'

'Fuck me now!' you demand.

There's the rip of plastic and foil, which must be the condom packaging, and then there's a long pause. You squirm, knowing that he's prolonging the moment, wishing one of your hands were free so that you could grab his cock, feel the solid strength of it, then guide it seamlessly inside you.

Then at last the tip of him is nudging up against your pussy, and you gasp with surprise and pleasure as his hardness pushes into you, stretching you to your limit. He pulls all the way out of you almost immediately, waits for a beat, then thrusts into you all at once again, as deep as he can go. Then he holds himself there, not moving, filling you entirely, completely, massively.

You feel him pull slowly out of you, but only partly this time, and then he rams his cock deep back inside. You gasp at the force of his penetration: if it wasn't so pleasurable, you're sure it would be painful.

Once again he pulls halfway out of you, and then waits for a couple of seconds. You thrash your head from side to side, trying to anticipate what's coming next, desperate for him to build up a rhythm, arching your back as far as you can in your restraints.

'Do you want me to go faster?' he asks.

You nod your head urgently.

'Say it,' he says.

'Go faster,' you plead.

'No, not yet,' he teases, just pressing the tip of his cock inside you. You move your hips, trying to capture his cock, to coax it further into you, but he evades you, withdrawing slightly, so you stop and wait for him to give it to you again, and by now you're frantic.

'Please ...' you whisper. And then you scream softly at the jolt of pleasure as he finally thrusts all the way back inside you.

And then at last he starts fucking you, first with a tantalisingly slow rhythm, then building up speed. You don't recognise your own voice as you hear it begging for more. At last, just as you can no longer stand his teasing, he slips into the perfect rhythm of long, patient thrusts. A massive orgasm gathers in your pelvis, and finally it reverberates through you, your body thrashing against the restraints.

In the hush that follows, Sven moves back on to his

knees between your legs, his cock still hard against your thigh. After a minute, hands loosen the restraints first at your feet, and then at your wrists, and you reach up to remove your blindfold.

'Don't!' Sven instructs, rolling you over on to your stomach. It's a relief to be able to move, so you kneel and flaunt your pussy at him.

He's behind you in a heartbeat, running his cock between your wet pussy lips, so the head grazes against your swollen, pulsing clit. Then he grabs your hips and slides his cock inside you, and it's an entirely different feeling at this angle, as he hits your g-spot with every movement. You've already come, so his rhythm is now for his own benefit, and you push back and clench against his thrusts, eager to push him over the edge. This is fucking, proper hard fucking, and it feels so good after all the teasing.

Sven clasps your breast as he comes, and you close your legs, tightening against his cock to heighten his orgasm, but as you squeeze your pussy, you're ambushed by a second orgasm. You push your bottom back up against him and reach for your clit with your fingers, sending yourself over the edge straight after him, your pussy clutching and releasing repeatedly around his cock. You feel a bead of his sweat drop on to your back and then you both collapse on to the bed, panting.

You pull the blindfold off your face, and blink in the dim light of the bedroom. Fucking hell, you think as a series of aftershocks chase through your body, you can't go wrong with the sights and sounds of Amsterdam.

THE END

'Oh yeah, baby, yeah baby … that's the spot …' Sven pants. 'A little to the left, okay, more, more, don't stop, that's so good …' His voice is gruff with pleasure. 'Harder, harder … now softer, softer.'

'Shhhh,' you say. 'I can't hear.' He quietens and you shift on his bed, nestling comfortably against the down pillows as you continue tickling his back with your fingernails. 'I can't believe your wildest fantasy is to lie on your bed and watch *Project Runway* while I tickle your back.'

'That's just the first part of my fantasy,' he says.

'What's the second part?' you ask as Heidi Klum intones, 'In fashion, one day you're in, and the next day you're out.'

'*Auf Wiedersehen*, Heidi,' Sven says, clicking the remote to turn off the TV. He rolls over to kiss you, running one hand down the length of your body, as the other closes around your breast.

'Aha,' you say, smiling up at him. 'I get the feeling it involves a little in-and-out of our own.'

EIND

You've decided to go to Venice to meet the Count

You exit Marco Polo airport into the soft Italian night, your stomach in knots at the prospect of meeting Claudio. You have to admit that you're a little hurt he didn't offer to pick you up. But you've done your homework, and as it's already pitch-dark outside, you've decided to take a water-taxi, even if it is very pricey.

By the time you get from the main airport buildings to the docks, you're cursing your suitcase – even with wheels, it feels as if you're dragging a baby elephant behind you. But you wanted to be prepared for every occasion, so you packed nearly all your party outfits and a ton of heels. You stagger down to the first mooring you see and give your destination to a hefty bloke at the wheel of a water-taxi. He reaches casually for the baby elephant, and you gulp as he heaves it over the side of the boat – you can't see the water, only blackness, but you can hear it slopping and smell its marshy tang.

The suitcase makes it into the boat okay, and then it's your turn. You discover there's no graceful way to step down into a gently rocking boat, and settle for a wobbly hop and scramble. The driver revs the engine and roars off into the night. Soon a scribble on the horizon resolves into a cluster of towers casting puddles of gold on the lagoon. Venice at last! In spite of your fatigue and nerves, you can't help feeling a thrill as you approach the island. Buildings loom and then your boat slips into the city like a needle, puttering slowly down a canal. You pass pontoons and steps where the sea seamlessly transitions to stone, mysterious gates and shadowed walls pressing close on either side until you emerge into a broader canal, glittering with soft lights.

'Grand Canal,' your driver says, dodging round a gondola, a clutch of motorboats and a waterbus with the ease of long practice. You turn again and the boat threads its way down another secretive channel. After only a few metres, it slows and bumps up against a set of steps, the driver rapidly throwing a rope around a mooring post. He hefts your suitcase out on to the narrow ledge between the buildings and the water, and clearly expects you to follow it.

'Er, is this the Palazzo Grania?' you ask nervously.

He nods, gesturing at the façade looming above you. Okaaaay … You pay him a faint-inducing amount of money, and in seconds he's unroped his boat and disappeared. Now what?

You peer at the walls, trying to find something like a name-plate or number, but no joy. This is all very atmospheric, but why doesn't anyone tell you that the one thing you need in Venice after dark is a good torch?

You notice that there's a little dog-leg around the building, and venture down it. It leads to an ancient wooden door, and next to it, what looks like a buzzer. At last! You press it, your nerves fizzing.

There's a long wait, then a crackle of Italian through some sort of loudspeaker. You jump and babble, 'Hello, it's me – hello, hello, Claudio, is that you?'

The door clangs open on to a dark courtyard, and you step inside. You can see a shape on the other side, turning keys – are you going to see Claudio in the flesh at last?

The man who comes out to meet you is a total stranger, a bear of a man with an impassive face and hooded eyes. He seems puzzled by your appearance.

'Hello,' you say, a little breathless. 'I'm here to see Claudio Lazzari.' Wait, should you use his title?

'Count – I mean *Conte* – Claudio Lazzari, *per favore*,' you say more firmly. 'He's expecting me.'

The man holds the door open and gestures to you to go inside, but makes no move to pick up your suitcase, and you can't face lugging it up the stairs, so you leave it in the courtyard and walk up and through the doors. Inside, you get a swift impression of rather chilly grandeur, as you face a pillared marble staircase.

'*Un momento*,' says your escort, disappearing into the recesses of the house. There's another agonisingly long pause, and then you hear footsteps above.

And this time, it really is Claudio who emerges – wow, he's even more stunning in the flesh than in his photos. He's not quite as tall as you'd imagined, but his dark hair and eyes are unmistakable, as is the cleft in his chin. He's coming down the stairs at speed, broad shoulders under his white shirt tapering to a dancer or athlete's hips, legs sheathed in perfectly cut suit trousers.

You beam up at him, but he doesn't smile back, and you feel a flicker of disquiet. Which turns to full-blown horror at his opening words: 'Good evening. May I help you?'

'Claudio!' you stutter. 'It's me. Glow Girl? Did you forget I was arriving tonight?'

He peers at you, his face a complete blank. Either he's a world-class actor or he really has no idea who you are. 'I'm very sorry, but I don't believe we've met.'

You flounder. Not in your worst nightmares did you envisage this scenario. 'Well, no, we haven't, but we've been chatting for weeks ...'

'Chatting? I'm afraid there's been some mistake.'

'You know, on pickmydate.com.'

He frowns. 'I don't understand. What is this pick-mydate?'

It's late, you've been travelling for hours, you've come all this way to see the guy after he pleaded with you to do so, and now either he's playing a hideous game or you've plunged into some bizarre parallel universe.

'Claudio, please. I'm the one that doesn't understand. We met online and we've been chatting and, er, other things ...' – you blush as you remember some of those things – 'for a while now, and you invited me out here to meet you ...'

His face remains stony, and by now your confusion is turning to alternating waves of anger and embarrassment. A handsome Italian Count wooing you, inviting you to stay at his seventeenth-century palazzo in Venice – you should have known it was too good to be true.

Claudio comes a little closer. 'There really has been some misunderstanding. I have no idea who you are, and I've never heard of pickmydate. Is it an internet dating site?'

You nod, wordless with mortification.

'So you got on a plane and came to see me, just like that? My God, have you never heard of frauds – what do you call them – scammers? It could have been anyone using my picture!'

Anger elbows embarrassment aside. 'You asked me to come! How do you think I got this address? And I'm not stupid, I checked you out. You're all over Google and Wikipedia, along with photos, lots of them – at Cannes, Monaco, on Lake Como, and even in this palazzo, your ancestral home. It all fitted with the things you were telling me, some of it personal stuff.'

A thought strikes you. 'Wait – didn't you have a big tabby cat when you were a kid? You called him Romeo because he used to meow under the balcony when he wanted to come in.'

Claudio gapes at you. 'Romeo? Yes ... yes, I did. How on earth do you know that?'

'See!' you shout, vindicated. 'You *told* me! No scammer would ever think of a detail like that. That's how I knew you were for real – along with the fact that you could spell. You're definitely the same guy as in those photos. I think you're the one playing me for a fool!'

Claudio stares at you for a long moment. Then, 'What name did you use when you looked me up?'

'Claudio Lazzari, of course. You can't deny that's who you are!'

Something flits across his face, and his mouth tightens. 'Ah, but I am not the only Claudio Lazzari. I have a thought. May I ask you to wait for one minute?'

But before he can move, someone else appears at the top of the stairs – an old man with bushy eyebrows and a walking stick. He leans over the banister and grins wolfishly down at you. '*Ciao, bella!* Welcome to Venice. Mmm, you're a pretty thing – even lovelier than in your pictures.'

Your sense of a parallel universe deepens. Has the entire world gone mad? Claudio races up the stairs and confronts the old man with a flood of rapid-fire

Italian. You watch as the two of them argue, the older shrugging and waving his arms about, the younger man visibly furious.

Eventually, Claudio turns to you. 'It seems the mystery is solved. Meet my father: whose name is also Claudio Lazzari. I owe you the most heartfelt apologies. I'm afraid he has played a terrible trick on you.'

'No trick!' cries Claudio Senior, and now that you know what to look for, the family resemblance is clear – the same slightly beaky noses and cleft chins, even the same mannerisms as they gesticulate at each other. But while Claudio's father still has most of his hair, even if it's snow-white, the chiselled jawline and voluptuous mouth have disappeared into a mass of folds and wrinkles, and the once-broad shoulders are stooped. You wonder fleetingly how Claudio feels, seeing his father and knowing exactly how he'll look in forty years' time, but you have much bigger worries.

The old man opens his arms beseechingly: '*Bella*, we have something special between us, do we not? I am so glad to see you. I intended to meet you at the airport, but my arthritis has been giving me some trouble.'

'You ... you catfished me!' At his son's puzzled expression, you add, 'It means deliberately misleading someone online, especially on dating sites, to create a fake relationship. It's a really low thing to do.'

Claudio Senior looks innocent. 'What can you possibly mean? We talked from and of the heart, you and I, we shared our secrets and desires, and things just happened.'

You all but choke. 'You said you were thirty-six years old!'

'Oh, everybody exaggerates a little on those sites, surely you know that?' The old rake leers at you. 'After all, you look as if you weigh a few pounds more than you said you did – but don't worry, I like it very much,' he says, carving an exaggerated hourglass in the air with his hands.

Claudio is caught between disbelief and fury: 'Is it true, Papa? You used my photos on an internet dating site?'

'So what?' There's a lot more shrugging. 'I looked exactly like you as a young man, and I still have the heart – and the passions – of my younger self,' he says, turning to you. 'And to think we made such sweet music together. Are you so horrified by my outward form? Surely it is the soul within that matters?' He gives you his best tragic look.

For a second, you're wrong-footed, but then fury surges up again. 'Wait a minute – you tricked me into coming all this way, to meet the wrong guy, and now you're trying to guilt me? You manipulative—' Words fail you, and Claudio steps in.

'Papa, your behaviour has been shameful, even if the young lady has been a little naïve. And now,' he continues smoothly as you shoot a glare at him, 'I think we should offer our visitor some hospitality, and make arrangements so that she can be as comfortable as possible. Shall we return to the family in the drawing room?'

Still seething, you follow the two men into a long room decorated with oil paintings and antique furniture. You're vaguely aware that the arched windows look directly on to the Grand Canal, but right now you're more concerned with the strangers looking quizzically at you.

Claudio makes the introductions: the silent man who let you in is topping up glasses, and you assume he must be the Italian version of the butler. You shake hands first with a ferociously stylish young woman, who is introduced as Adriana, a cousin who also acts as one of Claudio's personal assistants.

The person who makes the most vivid impression is the young man standing by the ornately carved fireplace. He has the same thick dark hair curling on his collar and beautifully formed mouth as Claudio, but his colouring is subtly different; his eyes are grey, not brown, and his freckled nose turns up slightly. He looks as if he finds the world a perpetual source of amusement.

'This is Van – short for Giovanni – my half-brother,' says Claudio.

'Hey, not so much stress on the "half"! It's lovely to meet you,' he smiles, turning up the charm wattage and reaching for your hand with both his. You don't miss that he runs his eyes swiftly up and down your body.

Claudio and his father speak excellent English, but with accents. Van, however, sounds English, and you comment on it.

'My mother – she was Papa's third wife – is English. We all went to English universities, but I went to English schools as well. Mum insisted.'

'I must warn you that where women are concerned,

Van takes after our father,' says Claudio, rubbing the bridge of his nose.

'That hurts, bro!' Van feints a mock-punch at Claudio, then addresses you. 'May I offer you a drink? You look like you might need one.'

You nod gratefully as he offers you a fluted glass of something grassy and fresh. 'Prosecco from our own vineyards,' he explains. You take a sip, and fragrant bubbles tickle your nose, cheering you.

'Vineyards in Venice?' you ask, and Van laughs. 'No, they're inland, about an hour's drive north. The family has a little vineyard on the Prosecco wine route. Now tell me, what's a lovely girl like you doing in a place like this?'

There's an electric pause. Claudio steps in: 'Our new friend is visiting for a ... holiday, but there's been a misunderstanding about her arrangements.' He turns to you. 'You must, of course, stay here.'

'I couldn't possibly!'

'Why not?' Van asks. 'There's loads of room. And Papa loves having visitors.'

'I do, I do, especially when they are *molto belle*,' Lazzari Senior smarms.

'We would be honoured if you would stay as our

guest and join us for a late supper,' Claudio says. 'But if the thought makes you uncomfortable, then of course we will find you a hotel. It is entirely your choice.'

'Please stay,' Van mouths. You hesitate – surely you shouldn't pass up the opportunity to stay in such a spectacular historic building? Then you glance at his father, who hasn't stopped ogling you. Spectacular palazzo or not, do you really want to put up with that old letch eyeing you all night?

If you decide to stay at the palazzo, go to page 126.
If you decide to take up Claudio's offer of a hotel, go to page 146.

125

'If you're sure it's not too much trouble ... I think I'd like to stay,' you tell Claudio.

'Excellent,' he says, then rattles out something in Italian to the silent butler. 'Your luggage will be taken to your room,' he says.

'Is there somewhere I can freshen up?' you ask.

Adriana gets to her feet smiling, but Van is there first. 'I'll show you to your suite,' he says. 'This way!' He crooks his arm for you to take, earning black looks from Claudio and his father. He leads you up another flight of stairs, and along a softly lit corridor.

'I'm so glad you decided to stay,' he says. 'Things could do with a little livening up around here.' He opens the door at the end of the passage with a flourish. Your mouth forms a silent 'O' as you take in an ornate four-poster bed, spread with a plum-coloured velvet coverlet. Gilt-framed watercolours and mirrors are ranged on colour-washed rose walls, and through a door, you catch sight of a pink marble bathroom.

'You'll enjoy it here, I promise,' Van says with another disarming grin. His cell phone beeps. 'Dammit. Got to take this. See you downstairs?'

The second he leaves, you sink on to the bed and gaze around at your surroundings, suddenly racked with doubt. Perhaps you should have gone to a hotel instead. You're way out of your comfort zone, and in a sense, you're staying here under false pretences. You jump at the sound of someone clearing his throat, and turn to see Mr Silent entering the room with your baby elephant.

'Your bag, *signorina*,' he says.

'*Grazie*. Do you speak English?'

'Of course. Is there anything I can get you?'

You shake your head, and he looks more closely at you. 'You are troubled?'

You sigh. 'A little. To be honest, I'm not sure I'm doing the right thing by staying here.'

'Come,' he says, striding over to the window, and opening the shutters with a flourish. You join him, marvelling at the night-time view of a turreted church flanked by palazzos, one with brickwork stained by centuries of water, the other adorned with faintly glimmering mosaics. Bells are chiming, the sound softened by water.

'This is what you are here for, is it not?' he says.

'I've never seen such a beautiful city.'

127

'But I understand why you are feeling unsure,' he says in a low and slightly husky voice that's at odds with the hard planes of his face.

'You do?'

He waves his arm around the room. 'If you are not born to it, this excess can be disconcerting. But you will get used to it, I am sure.'

You share a brief smile.

'Now, I must finish preparing the supper.'

'You're the chef?'

'I am many things, *signorina*,' he says. 'And hurry – your hosts may wait for you, but the food will not.'

With that, he glides out of the room, and you hurry into the bathroom to splash some water on your face.

The family is already seated when you make your way down to the dining room, and Van and Claudio leap to their feet as you enter. Mr Silent settles you in a chair at the head of the table (mercifully you're out of reach of Lazzari Senior) and pours you a glass of wine. As you take a sip of the rich white burgundy, Mr Silent sets a plate down in front of you.

'*Polenta e schie*,' Claudio says, 'baby shrimp on a bed of polenta. It is a local speciality.'

You taste it, the warm, buttery polenta melding

perfectly with the slightly garlicky and crispy shrimp. 'Delicious.'

'It's not the only delicious morsel at this table,' the old man says with a chuckle.

'Papa,' Claudio says warningly.

His father waves a dismissive hand and holds up his glass. 'To new friends!'

You all clink glasses and you start to relax. You were expecting the evening to be awkward, but you manage to hold your own in the conversation, which veers effortlessly from politics to pop culture, Van peppering his words with witty asides, his brother far more considered with his opinions. Only Adriana is silent, although you don't get the impression that she disapproves of you – every so often she gives you a small smile. As Mr Silent clears the plates and pours you all a glass of grappa, she excuses herself, saying she needs an early night.

'Why are you really here?' Van asks you, the second she's left the room. 'There's no way my brother could have kept someone as gorgeous as you a secret for so long, and Papa has been ogling you all night.'

You glance at Claudio and he lifts his shoulders. You take a sip of grappa, and the fiery liqueur slips down like burning silk, giving you courage. Van is bound to find out sooner or later. As you run through the whole sorry saga, you expect him to laugh or be aghast at your naïvety, but he listens in silence, scowling at his father every so often.

'Papa!' he says. 'You are incorrigible.'

'And I've been a complete fool,' you say.

'Nonsense!' the old man roars. 'Your only crime is that you are a romantic. And that is something one should admire in a woman.'

'I agree with Papa,' Van says, 'even if he is a randy old goat. Few people are willing to follow their heart's desire these days.' He meets your eyes, and you blush. You look up to see Claudio watching you, but you can't read his expression.

The randy old goat in question yawns and hauls himself to his feet. '*Signorina*, I wish I could apologise, but I cannot. If I had not brought you here, then we would all have been deprived of your company.' He shuffles over to you, and you manage not to wince as he kisses your hand. 'And now, I must retire.'

'Shall we go through to the library?' Claudio asks, as Mr Silent refills your glass. You banter with the brothers for a little while, then Claudio waves to a chess board in the corner of the room. 'Would you like a game?'

You shake your head and smother a yawn. The alcohol, your travels and the day's surprises are catching up with you. 'Maybe another time,' you say.

'I'll take you on, bro,' Van says. 'You owe me a rematch.'

You yawn again. Time to call it a night. Van jumps up and kisses you enthusiastically on both cheeks; his brother takes your hand and gently brushes it with his lips, sending a quiver through your body.

It's past midnight by the time you get to your room. You take a quick shower, wrap yourself in the silk robe left on the bed for you, and climb between the sheets, the linen so fine, it's almost glassy. It takes you ages to locate the light switch for the antique bedside lamp. The room finally in darkness, you lie back and replay the evening in your mind. All that grappa has left you a little flushed, but the surreal events of the night, the grandeur of your location, and the two impossibly handsome brothers have also played their part, and as you doze off, you're hyper-aware of your skin under the brush of the sensuous silk and the cool sheet.

There's a soft knock on the door. You fumble for the light switch, but can't find it. Moonlight shimmers into the room, and you can see just enough to tiptoe to the door without falling over anything.

'Who is it?'

'It's me.'

'Me who?'

Silence. Is it Van, or Claudio? You reach for the door handle, and then draw back. Are you really going to let a man you've only just met into your room? That would be reckless – and possibly crazy. But then again …

If you open the door, go to page 133.
If you don't open it, go to page 144.

You open the door

'Who—?' But before you can say another word, strong, warm fingers reach for your hand, and draw it against firm lips.

The moon has drifted behind a cloud, and all you can make out is a tall, dark silhouette. A pair of muscled arms wraps you in a gentle embrace, and you can't help letting yourself soften against the broad chest. You hold your breath – you know you should disentangle yourself, or at least find out whose body you're leaning against – but you're waiting to see what happens next. Lips brush against your temple, then against your ear, making you shiver. Your nipples harden against your mystery suitor's chest.

You open your mouth to say something at the same moment the lips travel from your ear across your cheek – and you hesitate, reluctant to break the spell. Then warm lips wrap themselves around yours, and you find yourself kissing your midnight visitor until you're dizzy. The only sound in the room is your quickened breathing – you're afraid that speaking will disperse the magic, and you'll find yourself in a fleapit

133

motel with a pumpkin and a cage full of mice, plus one toad.

You sway, and your suitor immediately lifts you off your feet, and deposits you gently on the bed. He doesn't follow you down, and you're relieved – and then a little disappointed. You can't see anything except a slightly denser patch of shadow hovering over you. The edges of your robe slide apart, and a finger runs down the length of your body. You wriggle, every atom of your skin leaping to attention, wanting more. Where will he touch – or kiss – you next?

After a pause just long enough to tantalise, you feel breath on your belly, followed by a slow lick around your navel. You moan and shift against the sheets. Then a mouth kisses you tantalisingly, just below one breast. By now, you're twitching with lust, all concern about who the mouth belongs to overtaken by anti-cipation of what it is going to do next. You're not disappointed: you feel breath fanning across your thigh, and you slide your legs apart in silent invitation. Everything is moonlight and slow motion – the warm breath between your legs, teasing, your body curving and spreading on the huge bed, the warmth blooming in your pussy, which is aching for contact.

Then a warm, wide tongue strokes confidently down your labia, parting the lips effortlessly, and you utter a small scream. The tongue stills and withdraws slightly, and you murmur, 'Don't stop!' And then the mystery mouth resumes its attention to your most intimate bits, licking with maddening slowness, sucking at your pussy lips, sliding in and out and around your folds, but not touching your clit. Time stretches as the tongue explores and laps, the sounds of wet meeting wetness intensely intimate.

There's no other point of contact between your bodies, but then a warm pair of hands slides gently under your buttocks, tilting your hips slightly upwards. It's followed by a tongue sliding in and up, penetrating you surprisingly deeply, thick and warm and wide, fluttering inside your pussy. You clutch at your breasts, rubbing against your erect nipples with your thumbs, and still you're unable to speak, caught in the spell of that mouth, the face only dimly sensed as it presses up against your rocking pelvis, a slight sense of stubble against your soft inner thighs.

The pleasure is acute, but not urgent, and also slightly surreal – the disembodied mouth worshipping your most private parts, creating the most thrilling sensations – you don't ever want this to end.

The tongue finally, reluctantly, withdraws from your pussy and travels languidly upward, and you cry out again as it comes to rest, hard and soft at the same time, against your clit, which is throbbing and super-sensitive. Then it begins to describe lazy loops and circles, sometimes with the hard tip, sometimes in broad sweeps. Pleasure begins to spiral inside you, your body tightening. But the unhurried tongue slows and teases, circling away and then back, and you give yourself over to its ministrations, letting the owner set the pace.

The pressure in your pussy and the surrounding muscles builds and builds, and you almost sob as the magical mouth slides down again, tonguing inside you in slow rhythmic thrusts. If you're ever allowed to come, it's going to be earth-shattering – you're beside yourself, making inarticulate noises, your head turning from side to side on the pillow.

Then, at last, the tongue licks firmly back up on to your swollen clit and laps harder and faster, still faster, and you can feel the explosion coming, and then you're screaming in earnest as your long-delayed orgasm floods through you, your body curving in ecstasy. You flood with fresh moisture, and a drum-beat hammers out from your pussy through the rest of your body, leaving you as limp as a kitten.

Vaguely, you're aware of the mouth pressing soft kisses on your thighs, then on your tummy. And then the shape withdraws altogether. 'Wait – what ...' you murmur, but the only response is the soft click of the door closing.

What just happened? You try to puzzle it out, but you can't fight the combined effects of travel, shock, the fiery liquor and now the satisfaction of a monster orgasm still pulsing through your lower body, rendering your arms and legs cotton-wool. You drift off as you're still trying to work out the identity of your mystery oral expert.

After sleeping like the proverbial baby, you head down to breakfast, still puzzling over the events of the night before.

You find Claudio alone in the dining room, paging through a document.

'How did you sleep?' he asks you.

'Fantastic,' you say, giving him a slow smile. 'Did *you* have a good night?'

137

He rubs a hand over his face. 'I confess I did not.'

You blanch. What can he mean? The only explanation is that it can't have been him who visited your room last night – it must have been his brother. You can't decide if you're relieved or disappointed.

Speak of the devil. 'Morning,' Van says cheerily. You look into his eyes, expecting to see a collusive glint.

'How can you look so fresh after last night?' Claudio grumbles.

You wince. Does he know his brother came to your room? How could he? Oh God ... but that would explain Claudio's grumpiness.

He turns to you: 'It's all your fault, you know.' You open your mouth, unsure how to answer, but he goes on, 'If you had agreed to play chess with me, I wouldn't have stayed up until the early hours doing battle with my brother.'

Van shrugs. 'What can I say? We're too evenly matched.'

Hang on. You glance at both of them. 'You mean ... last night you were playing chess together? Um ... without a break?'

Claudio sighs. 'Sadly, yes.'

Van looks at you quizzically. 'Are you okay? You look ... unwell.'

If it wasn't Van and it wasn't Claudio, that just leaves ... oh no. Claudio Senior. Surely you would have known if it was him? But then ... it was very dark.

'I ... I have to get out of here,' you say. 'I've made a terrible mistake.'

'Another one?' Van says.

'What do you mean?' Claudio asks.

'I need to leave. Right away.'

'Surely not?'

'Please,' you say. 'Can you call one of those water-taxis?'

'Hey—' Van starts.

'I don't want to talk about it,' you say, whirling out of the room. You run upstairs, zip up the baby elephant and haul it out on to the landing, stopping dead when you see who's standing in the hallway below.

'Good morning, *bella*,' Lazzari Senior smirks at you. 'How did you sleep?'

'How do you think I slept?' you snap.

He blinks, taken aback. 'I hope I did not disturb you last night?'

'"Disturb me?" Is that what you call it? Count Lazzari, I am more than just disturbed by your actions last night.'

'But I thought you had forgiven me for … let us just say, our little online misunderstanding?'

'You took advantage of me!'

'*Bella*, you are upset. And I must apologise. I tried to be quiet last night.' He taps his stomach. 'But I was up with indigestion all night. Rich food no longer agrees with me. Fortunately my sons were awake, and they kept me company.'

You look at him closely. He's certainly looking a little green around the gills. 'So you didn't come knocking on my door last night?'

He chuckles. 'Alas, I had not the strength for that.'

Claudio emerges from the dining room. 'We have a boat waiting to take you wherever you wish to go. I am sorry if we have offended you in some way. Goodbye.' With a curt nod, he stalks away. There's no sign of Van.

Still befuddled, and wondering if you've been the object of a giant practical joke, you dodge the elder Count's attempt to kiss you farewell, murmur garbled thanks for the night's hospitality, and then drag your suitcase into the courtyard and out the door that leads to the canal. Mr Silent is waiting for you outside, and at the sight of you, his impassive face breaks into a broad grin.

And then it hits you. 'You!'

Of course! It must have been Mr Silent. 'Last night. It was you!' You admit you were a more than willing participant, but the least he could have done was let you know his identity.

'But of course.' He frowns. 'You did not know this?'

'It was dark ... I ...' He's as tall as the Lazzari brothers, and just as fit – if not fitter. 'But ... I hardly know you!'

He tilts his head. 'Here is what you need to know. I have worked for the Lazzari family for five years. I am not married, I love to paint and read, and I adore to cook.'

He's certainly good at that, if yesterday's dinner was anything to go by. And that isn't all he's good at, you think, blushing as a scene from last night pops into your mind.

For a few seconds you stare at each other in silence. 'So what now?' you ask.

He smiles. 'That is your choice.'

141

You'd been planning to catch the next flight home, but then you gaze around Venice in daylight, really seeing it for the first time. There's something both timeless and magical about a city with no streets, floating on the sea, held together by canals, stone bridges and quays. And the constantly changing light – no wonder everyone raves about it. You're here now – it would be a pity not to explore. 'I suppose I'd better find a hotel.'

'I know somewhere you can stay. It's is not as luxurious as here, but it is very reasonable, and is the perfect place for you to explore all that Venice has to offer.'

'*All* that Venice has to offer?' You can't help smiling.

'That, *signorina*, is up to you. But if you are so inclined, perhaps I could take some time off and we could continue what we started last night?'

He reaches for your hand and breaks out the smile that transforms his face again, and you're suddenly flooded with optimism. Here you are in the most beautiful city on the planet, an undeniably sexy and very, very, er, *skilled* man looks delighted at the prospect of entertaining you, and who knows? There's a chance that your Venice adventure will have a happy ending after all – even if it's not quite the one you envisaged.

You squeeze his hand back. 'Why don't we start by telling each other our names?'

THE END

After a fractious night you've decided that it would be best to head to a hotel after all. You don't want to spend another night jumping at every sound in the corridor.

You find Claudio sipping an espresso in the dining room. If he was the one who came to your room last night, there's no sign on his face; he greets you with his usual gravitas. You explain that while you are immensely grateful for his hospitality, you've decided to stay elsewhere.

He immediately insists that you take one of the business suites kept for the family at the Hotel Danieli, ignoring your protestations. 'And while you are in Venice, you must see all that the city has to offer. I insist. Adriana will meet you at the hotel with a proposed itinerary for your stay here.'

He arranges for the hotel launch to collect you, and after a short and scenic boat ride down the Grand Canal and out into St Mark's basin, you arrive at the iconic dark-red hotel that will be your home for the next few nights. You can hardly believe your luck as you explore your suite, which gives your room back at the palazzo a run for its money in the luxury stakes. You unpack and then explore your new surroundings: the bathroom is more luxurious than most bedrooms, with a tub big enough to sleep in. You step out on to the balcony, and are watching the boats ply their trade on the silvery lagoon when the phone rings: apparently the efficient Adriana is waiting for you downstairs.

Go to page 157.

'Perhaps a hotel would be best, after all. Somewhere modest will be fine.'

'That will not be necessary. We have rooms held at the Hotel Danieli for our visitors, and the company settles the bills,' Claudio says definitely. 'Adriana, can you ring the hotel and check if the suite we use for business visitors is available?'

You start to protest, but Claudio shushes you with a motion of his hand. Adriana gets to her feet and walks towards the door, punching numbers into her mobile phone. She returns in minutes. 'It is all taken care of,' she announces. 'They're sending their launch – it will be here in twenty minutes. Do you have luggage?'

'Yes, still downstairs,' you say. The thought of a quiet hotel room is suddenly very appealing after the stresses and shocks of the evening.

Van pours you another glass of Prosecco, and by the time you've finished it, the hotel boat has arrived. You nod politely at everybody and sidle towards the door. Claudio Senior holds out his arms and puckers up roguishly: 'What, no goodnight kiss?'

You resist the temptation to flip him a finger, and scurry out, followed by Claudio, the butler, and Van's yelp of laughter. Claudio tucks a warm, firm hand under your elbow and escorts you down the stairs and out into the courtyard, where Mr Silent scoops up your suitcase as if it's packed with feathers and not your best finery. You sigh – not much chance of wearing any of that now.

Before handing you into the boat, Claudio looks into your eyes and apologises again. 'I really am sorry, from the bottom of my heart.'

'It's my fault too for being so impulsive. But it seemed like such a romantic thing to do, and it really did seem above board . . .' Your voice trails away. You can't believe you've been such a fool.

'Our family will make it up to you for putting you to so much trouble and expense,' Claudio goes on. 'Adriana will come to the hotel tomorrow with a suggested schedule so that you can at least enjoy your visit to Venice.'

Then, to your surprise, he leans forward and kisses you once on each cheek, before handing you into the boat.

The boat takes you down and out of the mouth of

the Grand Canal, with more landmarks gleaming with lamplight on either side – you recognise the great bubbles of the Salute church and the Customs House from your guidebook. Then you swing left and putter past St Mark's Square and the Doge's Palace. And isn't that the Bridge of Sighs, which Don Giovanni himself used for his trysts? It connects directly to a magnificent dark-red building with arched and pointed windows – the hotel itself, with ranks of gondolas moored outside and throngs of people strolling on the quays, even at this late hour.

You pinch yourself – you can't possibly be staying in a place like this! And yet the launch darts down a narrow canal and ties up at a side door, uniformed porters gathering to collect your luggage and help you out. They lead you into the vaulted lobby, the colours and opulent textures adding to your sense of being in a waking dream. Everywhere you look, you see Persian carpets with the patina of genuine age and silk, chandeliers like iced cakes and enormous artful flower arrangements.

You're ushered into an old-fashioned lift with red-flocked velvet walls, and, after a labyrinthine walk through stately drawing rooms and corridors – you don't know how you're ever going to find your way back out – you're shown to your suite. It's a sanctuary after the evening you've just had. That's if sanctuaries came with huge beds with padded tapestry headboards and handmade chocolates on the pillows.

If ever a bed was made for sex … but that option has gone out the window, along with your dignity. Sighing, you strip off your travelling clothes and pull on the luxurious towelling robe you find, before padding around to explore. You discover the minibar, discreetly set into the faux-medieval wardrobe, snag a dinky bottle of champagne and head for the bathroom. Which does not disappoint. Even in here, there are paintings on the walls and a luxurious armchair. The bath, set in cherrywood, is big enough for two people, and there's a cornucopia of cosmetic goodies.

Exactly what you need right now. You run a bath, decanting all the fragrant gels and oils you can find into the hot water, then climb in and lie back in a haze of steam and scent, the bubbly within reach. You've earned this, after the shock of discovering that you'd been tricked into visiting the wrong man.

You still can't believe it, you think, as you squeeze a sponge, trickling water between your breasts. When you think how you fantasised about making love to Claudio ... of being in a romantic setting like this one, of having him slip through the door, dressed only in a towel, dropping it to the floor and bending over you ... mmm. You stroke the sponge over your breasts, feeling your nipples grow tight, imagining those dark, deep-brown eyes gazing into yours ... and then a pair of grey eyes pops into your head.

Hey, what's that about? There's no doubt that Claudio is hot enough to melt lead, but now that you're thinking about it, his younger brother Van is also incredibly attractive. Given that you're going to be flying solo, does it matter who you pick to partner you in this dream setting?

If you decide Claudio's going to be your fantasy lover, go to page 151.

If you opt for a bold and breathless fantasy with Van, go to page 154.

You imagine a steamy scenario with Claudio

You lie back and imagine that Claudio's with you in the bathtub, that it's his firm chest you're reclining against. As you soak the sponge and hold it over your breasts, then squeeze, cascading warm water and scented froth over your skin, you picture Claudio's strong, tanned hands, the light sprinkling of dark hair on the back of his wrists.

You picture them wielding the sponge, running it over your breasts and nipples, cupping each in turn and rubbing gently. Then you move the sponge, and the image of Claudio's hands, slowly downwards ... the hot, slightly oily water feels so good, almost as good as the sponge, now underwater as it slides down over your tummy. You draw up one leg and rest it on the edge of the bath, then take a cake of luxury soap and lather up the sponge. Still holding the image of Claudio's hands in your head, you apply the sponge to your bush and rub in slow circles, opening your thighs even wider.

Lazily, luxuriously, you run a finger between your legs, delicately feeling for the slit. You're still picturing Claudio's agile fingers, and you gasp as you imagine

151

that's it's him parting your pussy lips, deftly pushing deeper, warm water bathing your own wetness and heat.

You wriggle in the silky, scented water, taking your time, exploring thoroughly before locating your clit. In your head, it's Claudio who's stroking around and across, before starting to rotate a fingertip on your clit with exactly the right amount of pressure – not too much, but not too tentative, either. You tilt your head back, imagining that it's his collarbone you're feeling, his warmth against your back.

Your breath is starting to come in pants as sensation radiates from your clit, creating that familiar tension in your pussy. Keeping a thumb on the outside, you imagine that the finger now sliding inside you is Claudio's, that he's murmuring encouragement as your pussy starts to pulse – and then you're coming in strong, utterly satisfying waves, and the water slops around as you thrash and groan.

Then there's that lovely hush in your body, all the tension of the day soaked out, and you're still lolling luxuriously in a huge bath in a fairy-tale hotel – with a glass of bubbles within reach. You sigh. You know you've just been fantasising, but stranger fantasies have become reality. Who knows what wishes might come true in this magical place? It's definitely worth sticking around in Venice for a few days.

Go to page 157.

You fantasise about a dalliance with Van

You get out of the bath, wrap yourself in the velvety robe, and google Van on your laptop. A row of thumbnail images pops up, and you click on them one by one. There's a shot of him playing polo with Prince Harry, and another of him about to bungee jump off a high bridge in South Africa, all teeth and tan – clearly he's a bit of an international playboy. This is interesting – a photo of him with his mother, watching Wimbledon together. You peer at them; she's very lovely, but she has that brittle and slightly glassy look that goes with long years of dieting and too much Botox.

You click around some more, and discover that Van is definitely single, if having strings of beautiful women in attendance and half-a-dozen rumoured affairs counts as unattached. It sounds like he's a bit of a bad boy, but that could be half the fun. You're sure he'd be up for some pretty wild stuff.

Naked under your luxurious robe, you open the window and step out on to the narrow balcony with a view over the water. There are still tourists lingering on the stone quay below, gondoliers poling in their crafts after the evening's trips, but the stalls selling tourist trinkets are closing up for the night.

You imagine Van in this suite, standing behind you, his hands reaching around your waist. You slide a hand under the fabric of your robe, and cup your breast. The air is soft, and surprisingly warm, and there's something wickedly taboo about touching yourself with strangers ambling around only yards below you.

Giving your imagination free rein, you visualise Van pressing against you from behind as you stand on the balcony, pushing up your robe, freeing his cock, pressing it against your thighs from behind. Anyone looking up at the pair of you would see only a tall man hugging a woman from behind – you're decent from the front.

You gaze out at the lights on the water, running a hand discreetly between the two sides of the robe, opening your legs a little, imagining Van's warm velvety cock nudging at you. Your hand creeps between your legs – your X-rated imaginings have made you spectacularly wet, and you gasp as your finger slides up into your pussy.

You can't believe you're touching yourself like this

almost in public – it makes you feel wild and free and incredibly aroused. But you're not up for having an orgasm in public – yet – and so you step back from the balcony, imagining Van pulling you towards the enormous bed, his erection straining with need. You throw yourself backwards on to the bed, pull your legs up and finger-fuck yourself, imagining him rolling on the bed with you. As you picture yourself straddling his body, mounting his cock, drawing it triumphantly inside you, you start coming in short, fierce bursts, groaning with relief. Wow, you were way more tense than you realised, you think, as your breathing starts to slow. Strangely enough, a quick and dirty orgasm was just what you needed, and you grin to yourself, feeling a bit more optimistic. You think you'll be ready to face Venice tomorrow – and although you're sure to blush if you see Van again, you're kind of hoping it happens …

Go to page 157.

You've decided to stay in Venice

The vista across the lagoon, the misty light touching the water with pearl and faint lemon, makes you want to linger on your balcony. But Adriana is waiting for you in the hotel's plush downstairs sitting room. She's dressed for business in an impeccable suit and scarf, and orders camomile tea for herself and cappuccino for you. You're still trying not to gawp at your surroundings – you're sure that's a minor film-star sitting at the table next to yours, but you don't want to stare too openly.

'I have drawn up several options for you to consider,' Adriana says, opening a folder that contains a map of the city, a vaporetto pass and several museum passes. 'As this is your first visit to Venice, you most probably want to start by seeing the Piazza San Marco and the Doge's Palace. Tomorrow, there are the galleries and also the islands – I am happy to act as your guide. Or maybe you would like to go to Nice? Claudio has a business meeting there that will take most of the day, so he's taking the company jet.'

You're confused. 'Why Nice? I mean, it sounds lovely, but what would I do there?'

'Claudio is a personal friend of the Director at the perfume museum situated in the mountains outside the city. He thought you might like to do a workshop there. The perfumer helps you to blend your own personal scent – it takes several hours, and they give you lunch and champagne. It's a nice way of spoiling yourself, and very interesting, too.'

She pauses to look at her folder. 'We would also like to invite you to a private opera soirée, a performance at one of the palazzos – that's the night after tomorrow. You must come to that, it will be so much fun!'

Her professional mask slips as she leans towards you, animated. 'It's a family tradition, our own small carnival. We all dress up in costume and wear masks, a rehearsal for the big parties and balls that come with the *Carnevale* at the end of winter. Opera is a big part of the carnival, the singers and musicians perform in the big palazzos, the champagne flows, and afterwards we dance till dawn. It's wonderful. So we allow ourselves a little taste of it before the winter begins.'

Hmm. You packed your favourite little black dress, along with a red chiffon number suitable for cocktails or dinner, but you're not sure if that's what one wears

to a costumed opera outing. 'I'm not sure I have anything suitable to wear.'

'That is easily solved. There are shops that hire out
costumes – I'll take you to visit one. You'll have to get
a mask, perhaps a wig, too, if you like – it depends on
what costume you choose. We take it all very seriously – we get in professionals to do our hair and
makeup, we even hire jewellery if necessary.'

She taps at the folder on the table before you. 'But
what would you like to do in the next two days? I am
at your disposal.'

Now that you've decided to stay for a few days,
even after the debacle of the double Claudios, you're
rather enjoying having choices. Should you focus on
the magical sights of Venice?

Or why not take a trip to Nice and see a bit of the
Riviera (and a bit more of Claudio), since you have
the opportunity? You rather like the idea of a perfume
workshop – you've always loved gorgeous fragrances,
and it would certainly be something different.

If you decide to explore Venice, go to page 160.
If you choose to fly to Nice with Claudio, go to page
   183.

You've decided to *wander round Venice*

It's a beautiful day, with balmy early-autumn weather
and a low ceiling of cotton-wool cloud letting in the
odd shaft of sunlight, making the faded reds and
ochres of the buildings glow. You've elected to stroll
around on your own – you're sure Adriana has better
things to do than babysit you – and you've braved the
crowds feeding pigeons in the Piazza San Marco and
queuing to go into the Basilica and the exquisite
Doge's Palace, which makes you think of Turkish
Delight, with its pink patterning. Now you're just
wandering around, getting repeatedly lost – it's all
very well following the map, but you keep running up
against dead ends and little canals and having to
retrace your steps.

Your visit has coincided with the Venice Biennale, a
massive international art jamboree. You're not usually
an art freak, but there's so much lovely and unusual
stuff to see, often in strange combinations, and you're
having fun strolling into Renaissance churches to find
angular modern figures sculpted from rusty metal rubbing up against the usual residents: centuries-old
statues of podgy cherubs and sad-eyed saints.

You find yourself on the southern side of the Grand Canal, on the wide stone quay known as Zattere, where there are fewer tourists and more of a student crowd. You sit down on a flight of steps outside a church to watch a gigantic cruise ship being nudged along the channel by a tough little sheepdog tugboat.

The sun is warm enough to feel pleasant on your face, and you're shamelessly basking when a tall young man all but falls over you as he emerges from the church doors.

'*Scusi, signorina*, I'm so sorry!' he says – is that a slight American accent?

'No problem,' you reply. The sun is in your eyes, and you blink – he's just a silhouette against the light, but as he comes into focus, you blink again. He's one of the most striking men you've ever seen. Like Venice itself, all the most attractive elements of both east and west blend in his face. His eyes and wing-shaped brows slant upwards in parallel with cheekbones you could use to rule lines, and he has long shining black hair tucked behind his ears, hanging loose to his shoulders.

He's tall and very thin, with that slightly loose-jointed frame that always looks so sexy in motion.

Smiling, he offers you a huge but beautifully shaped hand, with prominent wrists and long fingers.

'You speak English!' he says, folding himself down gracefully next to you. 'I'm sorry, it's pitch-dark inside and for a second, I couldn't see as I stepped out. Mind if I join you? The name's Zhou.'

You spend a few minutes exchanging getting-to-know-you details, and you establish that he's an artist who's staging an exhibition in this church. His mother is Chinese, his father is Iranian, he studied art at Berkeley, and now lives in San Francisco.

He's familiar with Venice, and it's great to have someone to ply with questions about the place – he's certainly less intimidating than the polished Adriana. He tells you about the little bars and bakeries where you can eat the same food the locals do, and how to read the vaporetto route maps, which look like you need a degree from MIT to decipher them.

'Is there a single ordinary building in Venice?' you ask, and he laughs.

'It is a bit of a living museum. Sadly, not many locals can afford to live here – many of the folk who work here, in the restaurants and shops, live on the mainland and commute here daily. But it's still the most beautiful and romantic city in the world.' He turns those slanting eyes on you. 'Speaking of romance, do you mind me asking if you're here alone? Or do you have a beefy boyfriend back at your digs?'

You're sharply reminded of the ridiculous tangle you've managed to get yourself into, and can't help drooping. 'Oh no, I've put my foot in it, haven't I?' says Zhou. 'I'm sorry, I didn't mean to pry. I just wanted to show you round my installation and maybe go for a drink afterwards, but I didn't want to make any assumptions.'

'It's a long and very silly story, but the short answer is that I'm here alone, even if that wasn't the initial plan,' you sigh.

'In that case, how about a guided tour of my exhibition? I promise you don't have to make admiring noises. If you hate it, you can always develop a tactful coughing fit.'

'Why not? I don't have anything else planned.' Secretly you hope his art isn't the kind of avant-garde work where stuffed animals are suspended in jelly or a broken clothes-peg is stuck in a huge frame with a title like *Domestic Rhapsody #13*. But you're not about to turn down an invitation from a guy who's even better-looking than the Renaissance statues of angels you've been seeing all day.

You let him tug you to your feet and lead you into the church – where at first you can't see anything. Zhou explains that because some of the works take the form of videos, the exhibition space is kept dark, and on cue, a spangle of lights begins to dance on the floor in front of you, like multicoloured fireflies. It's pretty, and you say so.

You proceed down the nave of the church to the altar, which is the main exhibition space. Here paintings of various sizes hang from fixed metal struts or chains suspended from the ceiling – some revolve, revealing pictures on both sides. Spotlights pick out the images, which are dream-like – a seagull flies through the depths of the ocean, dwarfing a whale; a horse stands looking over the shoulder of an old man reading a newspaper on a bench; a child plays solitaire on a laptop that dissolves into a galaxy.

'These are lovely!' you whisper, and you're rewarded with a squeeze, Zhou's long fingers brushing the skin of your shoulder.

'I want to show you my favourite,' he says. 'But for that we need to sit down.'

You sit down on the altar steps, curious, and Zhou tells you to look up. There, projected on to the dome of the church, is a video of clouds streaming across the sky, making it look as if the top of the building has been opened up by a celestial tin-opener.

As you watch, the clouds turn into fish swimming through blue water, seaweed rippling in an endless current. The starfish passing across the dome slowly turn into real stars, as the water deepens into mid-night-blue sky ... and then the stars fade, the sky goes gilded pink and the cycle repeats. It's strangely moving, and as you turn to tell Zhou how much you like it, your eyes fill with tears.

'Hey, hey, what's the matter?' he says, and the concern in his voice undoes you.

'It's all such a mess – I've been such a fool.' You swipe away the tears, furious at yourself for letting the shocks of the previous night affect you so deeply.

'Boyfriend trouble?' Zhou cocks his head.

'"Imaginary boyfriend trouble" is more like it.'

Zhou reaches for your hand. 'Look, I don't know exactly what's upsetting you, or how serious it is, but I know something that can cure almost anything in the world.'

'Including making a complete, spectacular, monumental idiot of yourself?' you sniffle.

'Especially that. C'mon!' he says, and you let yourself be escorted out of the church, round the corner, along a narrow canal where two gondoliers are polishing the brasses on one of their boats – and your destination becomes clear.

'Tah-dah!' sings Zhou, looking pleased with himself – and well he might. The man is a genius, and not just as an artist. The sign on the tiny shop in front of you spells the fabled word GELATO, and you feel better already.

'It's on me,' says Zhou. 'I recommend the pistachio flavour.'

Five minutes later, you're strolling next to the canal, eating the most decadent ice-cream you've ever encountered. Something about the gentle sun, the exotic setting, the art you've seen – which makes you feel as if Zhou's not a stranger, but someone whose inner workings you've glimpsed – prompts you to start telling him your story. Or maybe it's the magic of Italian ice-cream.

Either way, it feels good to get it off your chest, and Zhou is a great listener – he makes sympathetic and horrified noises in all the right places as you explain how your great romantic rendezvous went belly-up. As you wind up your tale of woe, you peep at his face – is his mouth twitching?

'You're laughing at me!'

'I'm not, I swear!' he says, but his eyes keep tugging at the corners, and as the absurdity of it all hits you, you burst out laughing. Once you start, you can't stop, and soon the pair of you are leaning against each other, near hysterical with mirth.

'Oh God, that dirty old man!' you hoot. 'You couldn't make something like that up!'

'I think after that story, you deserve a lick of my cone,' says Zhou. 'I promise it's absolutely delicious.'

'Really?' You lean towards him. 'Are you going to lick mine, too?'

Your eyes meet and hold as you stand on tiptoe and take a slow lap at the remnants of his ice-cream. As you do, he licks it as well, and the realisation that your tongues are less than an inch apart sends an angel dancing down your spine. You both lick again, slowly, almost in unison. If you go on doing this, in a few seconds you'll be kissing, and the thought makes your knees wobble.

You steady his cone with your fingers, sliding them between his as he holds it, and some of the melting confection runs down on to your hand.

Still gazing into your eyes, he lifts your fingers with his free hand, and delicately laps the melting ice-cream from them. Then he captures your forefinger, pulls it into his mouth, and sucks. You shiver – which he notices – and then you both lean in for the last mouthful of his cone – and find each other's lips, still chilled and sweet from the ice-cream.

You hold the remnants of your own cone away from your body as Zhou folds his arms around you, anchoring you firmly as he explores your mouth with supple lips. His timing is perfect – just as you start wanting more depth from the kiss, his tongue presses against your teeth, and you open up to him, tipping your head back, relishing the different textures, the softness of his tongue, the smoothness of his lips, the slight grain of stubble as he angles his head to kiss you more deeply.

One of his hands slides down to your bottom and the other is travelling across your upper back – you've both dropped your cones – and you're kissing each other with deepening eagerness. And then Zhou swings you round, slings an arm across your shoulders and starts almost running back towards the church. You stumble up the steps, back into the gloom, past his paintings, and into a side-chapel.

You can barely see him in the dark, but you can feel his hands clasping your face, and then his mouth is on yours again, and you're kissing each other almost ferociously. Next minute, you feel his hand on your thigh, sliding up under your skirt with intent. Wow, this guy doesn't hang about!

You're momentarily unsure – kissing is one thing, but shagging – and in a church? Won't that get you hit by lightning or something?

'Wait,' you say, drawing away a little.

'Too fast?' Zhou pants. 'Or is the location a problem?'

You think for a second. It's a bit of both, really. But maybe this is exactly what you need to wash away the taste of your humiliation at the hands of the Lazzaris. There's no denying that you find Zhou incredibly attractive (you have a pulse, after all). He's gorgeous, an artist, and he has perfect instincts when it comes to ice-cream. Perhaps you should jump at the opportunity – and jump him, too.

If you decide to throw caution to the winds and shag in the church, go to page 171.

If you'd prefer somewhere a little more private (and less sacrilegious), go to page 173.

You wind your arms around Zhou's neck and kiss him firmly. 'I'm game,' you whisper into his ear, before nibbling on the lobe. That should send the message loud and clear, and he groans and nuzzles your neck as one hand comes up to cup first one breast, then the other, strong fingers working at your nipples. His other hand keeps smoothing up and down your spine as he walks you backwards until you feel cool stone behind you.

Then his hand is warm on your thigh, reaching higher and higher, up towards your hip. You feel his fingers hook into the lace of your knickers and tug firmly. This is really going to happen, and as his mouth travels down your neck in the direction of your breasts, you let your head fall back.

You almost shriek aloud – a pair of mournful eyes is gazing down at you. They belong to a Madonna whose look of deep sorrow at the general wickedness of humanity has lasted for several centuries, but the effect on you in the here and now is instant.

'Zhou, I'm so sorry, I can't do this – at least not here!' You disentangle yourself, panting.

He immediately slackens his grip and starts to

apologise. 'You're right – maybe this isn't the most relaxing setting,' he says, his own breath still coming in ragged gasps. 'I have an idea ...'

It crosses your mind that you could always go back to your hotel, but it's the other side of the Grand Canal, and you're not sure the moment between you will survive a long hike or a trip on a crowded vaporetto.

'Got somewhere a little less, um, sacred in mind?' you ask. 'Preferably with no dead saints or holy virgins checking us out?'

Go to page 173.

You've decided to find somewhere more private

You follow Zhou along more of the narrow lanes called *calles* and across a network of tiny stone bridges until you come to a low doorway that leads into a lobby with the inevitable black and white marble mosaic floor. Signs indicate that this is yet another installation for the Biennale – one of the Central Asian republic's exhibits.

A young man is dozing at the entrance desk, and he barely cracks an eye open as he nods at Zhou, who whisks you past. You head up a flight of stairs, past brightly coloured sculptures and wall-sized photographs of a gypsy wedding. Finally Zhou holds aside a red curtain and gestures you to step inside a small room.

Amazing – you've entered what looks like a sultan's tent. The entire floor is carpeted in a rug richly patterned in red, gold and black. The pattern has been repeated on fabric and painted on to wood so that the entire room replicates the carpet – the walls, the woven draperies hanging from the ceiling, the cushions, the furnishings. It's the most sensuous room imaginable – even if it does look a little like you imagine an acid trip feels – and you have it entirely to yourselves.

Zhou draws you down on to the cushions and immediately starts tugging at the zip of your dress.

'Hey,' you say, capturing his hand. 'We don't have a train to catch.'

'I know, I'm acting like a teenager,' he admits. 'It's just that you're so hot, I'm scared you'll evaporate.'

You can't help giggling. 'More of this, please,' you say, twisting a handful of his silky hair between your fingers and kissing him languorously. For what feels like an age, the pair of you entwine on the soft carpet and cushions, rolling over and over, locked together by mouth and tongue. Finally, you're the one who insists on removing your dress, pulling it up over your head, and giving his shirt the same treatment.

Zhou's lean, amber-coloured torso is smooth, hairless and silky to the touch. On the pectoral muscle over his heart is a tattoo of flowing lines, some kind of exotic writing. 'Is that Arabic? What does it mean?' you ask, tracing one of his small tight nipples with a finger.

'It's the word for "art" in Persian calligraphy script,' he says. 'I know it's a cliché, but it means that my heart really does belong to my art ... although right now, you're the work of art I'd like to focus on.'

It's a cheesy line, but you don't care as his fingers reach behind you to unhook your bra. He kisses your mouth once more, then his lips travel south, sliding down your neck, on to your collarbone, down towards the swell of your breast. You groan and bend your back, eager for the feel of his mouth on your nipple – and he doesn't disappoint you, sucking the entire tip of your breast slowly into his mouth, then circling your nipple with an agile tongue.

After a few minutes of heaven, you whisper, 'The other one's getting jealous,' and he laughs against your skin and transfers his attention to your other breast. This time when he slides his hand up your thigh, you're eager for it, lifting your hips as he hooks your knickers with a finger so that he can pull them off easily.

Momentarily, you have an out-of-body flash – you're stark naked in a foreign city, rolling around in the arms of a stranger, on a carpet that belongs in a sultan's harem. It seems Zhou is also taken by the picture you make – literally. He's pulled out his phone.

'You look so fantastic, those curves, that silky skin

against the fabrics and tassels and all that red and gold – can I photograph you?'

You gulp, visions of your naked body flashing around the internet filling your mind, but you're so aroused, it's hard to care. 'Okay, but don't include my face,' you say, and he takes the shot, then lies down next to you to show you the picture. You have to admit it looks fantastic – your body forms a graceful S-bend around a cushion, your skin shimmers against the rich colours and textures, and your breasts gleam.

'Time for you to get naked,' you whisper, attacking the button on his jeans. His legs go on for ever as they emerge from the denim, and he has a penis to match – it's slightly curved, and so hard, it's almost as if it's made from some kind of marble itself. But the dusky, moist head gives away that he's very much flesh and blood.

'Sauce for the gander,' you smile, reaching for his phone and pushing him down among the fabrics and rugs, then taking a cheeky shot that shows his cock rearing up from the smooth perfection of his hairless body, rather like one of the many pillars you've seen that day. 'Hey, it's the Leaning Tower of Venice!'

He grins, then props himself up on one elbow to

look at the picture you've taken. 'How about a little restoration work?' he whispers, taking one of your hands and wrapping it around his cock. You squeeze, and he moans, then rolls on to you and dips a knee between your legs.

You take the hint and part your legs, and then it's his turn to go exploring, his fingers drifting up your inner thigh. There's that delirious moment just before he makes contact with your pussy, when you're practically humming with want, and then you feel warm fingers grazing your lips, opening them, your wetness smearing on to your thighs, and then the jolt as one finger slides up inside you, and another rubs over your clit.

As you whimper in ecstasy, you feel warm hands pressing your thighs open, silky hair falling over your mound, and then his even warmer mouth comes down on to your pussy, sucking, his tongue sliding between and around your lips as one finger continues to slowly rub your clit.

It's almost too much, and you buck and squeal, biting your fist, wanting to slow down, but he's ruthless, the strong suck of his mouth alternating with the rhythmic press of his fingers, and you feel the helpless onset of an orgasm. It gathers force in your pelvis, then explodes through your body so sharply, it's almost painful, and you thrash against the cushions, your head jerking, crying out. The relief that follows is exquisite – you feel the tensions and disappointments of the past twenty-four hours melting as your body pulses, your heart rate gradually returning to something close to normal.

At last you open your eyes, to see Zhou rearing up over you, smiling, his cock still standing to attention. This is very far from being over, and as you lie sprawled wantonly in front of him, he reaches for his jeans and scrabbles in a pocket, fishing out a condom.

Then he turns you on to your tummy. You're too spent from the force of your orgasm to get into a kneeling position, but it seems that isn't what he has in mind. Instead, he drapes you over a pile of cushions so that your bottom is slightly raised and your thighs parted, your head resting on your arms.

You hear the rustle of the condom wrapper, and then his voice in your ear as he crouches over you: 'Are you ready for me?'

You murmur assent, and feel the tip of his sheathed cock nudging at the entrance to your soaking pussy, and then the glorious stretching sensation as he slides deep inside you. Even though you're boneless and drenched, your pussy takes a few seconds to adjust. The angle is new to you, pressing on nerve endings you didn't know you had, and you moan happily.

Zhou starts to thrust, slowly at first, almost more of a press, then pushing a little deeper on each stroke. You gasp each time he slides home, and then you hear him whisper: 'I'm filming this.'

What? That's not what you signed up for! But before you can protest, a long arm comes round you, holding the phone, showing you the clip he's just filmed. You watch mesmerised at the sight of his long, smooth, gleaming cock sliding into your deep-pink pussy, which looks like some juicy tropical flower, your lips wide open, wet everywhere, on your skin and his. It's shocking and hot at the same time, watching your cunt swallow his cock over and over, listening to your gasps and his groans, especially as he continues to thrust into you as you both stare at the phone screen, your movements and cries continuing, a kind of feedback loop of pleasure.

Zhou drops his phone, needing both hands to hold on to your hips as his thrusts come faster and faster. And then with an immense grunt, he comes, in four or five spasms, each one driving his cock deeper than the last.

There's a long pause as he pants into your neck, and then he collapses on top of you, and you give way beneath him, both rolling into the softness of the surrounding fabrics.

You keep clasping each other, but without urgency now, your bodies lightly filmed with sweat and satisfaction.

'I think we may have ruined the exhibit,' you murmur eventually, stretching a lazy hand out towards your bra, which is peeking out from under what looks like a camel's saddlecloth.

'Oh, it's surprisingly resilient,' he says, rolling on to his back to deal with the condom, then stretching out next to you.

You're struck by a thought, as you add it up – Zhou's familiarity with the location, the seen-it-all-before response of the bloke at the entrance desk, the convenient condom: 'I'm not the first woman you've brought here!'

He raises his hands in mock surrender. 'No, you're not the first girl I've brought here – or guy, for that matter. Why, is that a problem for you?'

You stare at him, disappointed, but also angry with yourself for feeling that way. It's not as if you have any claims on this guy – all you know is that he's scorchingly hot and talented, and he's made you feel better about yourself on a day when your self-confidence meter was set on zero.

You make up your mind. 'No, no problem at all. I can do time-share if I have to, and I've had a fantastic amount of fun. But there is one thing I'm not prepared to share ...' And you reach for his phone.

He watches wryly as you find the raunchy little porn clip of your bodies moving together, and watch it for a few reminiscent seconds. You really do look hot together. Then you delete it with a swipe. He yelps a bit, but he doesn't move to stop you.

You decide to spare the anonymous picture of your body curving among the cushions, and hand him back his phone. 'Right, that's done. Let's get dressed and go get a drink. All that exercise has made me thirsty.'

He helps you up and hands you your clothes. 'Yup, and the good news is that we burned off all that gelato. Just in case you want to get some more.'

As you stroll out together, your phone beeps. It's the super-efficient Adriana – she's left messages about the opera at the hotel, and wants to know whether you'll be able to find your way to the costume shop for a fitting the next morning.

'Zhou, this has been lovely, but I have to get back to my hotel and sort this out,' you say. 'Another time?'

'I'll take a rain check,' he smiles, unworried. 'You can always find me via my website. You never know, one day you might come into money and want to buy one of my pieces.'

'Deal,' you say, leaning up to kiss him. He walks you to the vaporetto stop, and as you board, you turn to see his loose-limbed body strolling through the crowds, his hands in his pockets. He looks back and waves, then he's gone. For the rest of your life, you'll think of him every time you eat pistachio ice-cream.

Go to page 203.

Claudio picks you up at the Danieli dock – you're not surprised to see Mr Silent at the helm of the motor-boat. You've already become blasé about travelling everywhere by boat, and you rocket off to the airport again. The security checks are over in no time, and you're looking forward to being alone with Claudio on the plane.

You've had time to lick your wounded pride, and you've decided that as you're here on his home turf, there's no reason not to get to know the guy better – or perhaps give him the chance to get to know you a little. He's as good-looking in real life as he is in his pictures, and according to the tabloids you Googled last night, he's not involved with anyone in particular. He's accompanied by beautiful women in some of the photos you found, but it's never the same one, and you recognised Adriana on the red carpet with him at the most recent film premiere at Cannes – attending with his cousin doesn't suggest that he's embroiled in a serious relationship.

You're probably the last woman on earth he'd be interested in, after the debacle of that first evening, but you have this day together, so why not make the most of it? You buckle up in the gleaming cabin – you've never been on a private jet before, and you're trying not to be too visibly awed – and slide him a look from under your eyelashes.

To your great disappointment, he opens up his briefcase and fishes out his tablet and a fat file of papers. 'I'm so sorry,' he says, 'I need to prepare for this meeting. These clients are very particular.'

Oh well. Fortunately, it's not a long flight, and you amuse yourself by alternately admiring the spectacular scenes of lakes and snow-covered mountains passing below, and reading the brochures the ever-competent Adriana has provided on your perfume workshop. It does sound intriguing.

Eventually the pilot announces that you need to prepare for landing. As the plane descends, you peer through the window at the Riviera, the mountains rearing up out of the aqua sea, the city of Nice a bowl of red and yellow sequins below you. It's one of those landings when it seems certain that you're going to splash down in the water, but at the last minute, the runway materialises under the wheels, and you touch down smoothly.

You're met by a chauffeur in a luxury car, and bowl along the beachfront, with its palm trees. Now that summer's over, the beautiful stretch of sand and sea is punctuated only by a handful of men with fishing rods and flasks.

Claudio gets out at the Méridien Hotel, where he'll be spending most of the day in a boardroom, but you continue up into the rocky hills. The gardens are lusher than you expected, with hedges of plumbago and bougainvillea enclosing olive and fig trees. Soon you crest a narrow neck, a tiny village of ancient stone perched on a rocky outcrop to your right, and your destination – the salmon-pink perfume museum – on the left. The chauffeur promises to fetch you at the end of the afternoon, and departs.

Your name generates a flurry of greetings and smiles – clearly, this time you're expected – and a pretty young woman in a black pinstriped suit escorts you deep into the heart of the building, past huge copper stills and posters showing workers knee-deep in roses and mimosa, shovelling the flowers into vats.

She ushers you into a room that manages to blend the feel of an old-fashioned apothecary's shop – shelves of tiny brown bottles with names like vetiver and ylang-ylang – with a modern chemical lab, complete with pipettes, measuring-tubes and sinks.

Your escort withdraws. A few minutes later, you hear the brisk sound of high heels coming down the passage, and a striking woman strides into the room. She's not conventionally pretty, but she has that unmistakable style and carriage for which Frenchwomen are famous. Her expertly coiffed red hair is cut into a razor-sharp bob, and the sage-green bouclé suit she's wearing can only be Chanel. Her exquisitely shaped legs end in simple but screamingly stylish high black heels, and the hand held out to you in greeting is impeccably manicured.

This is Madeleine, the Director of the museum and apparently also a master – or should that be mistress? – perfumer herself.

'*Enchantée*,' she says as you introduce yourself. 'Come, make yourself comfortable. Amélie will bring us coffee in a minute. I always enjoy working with individuals to create their own signature scent. And Claudio is an old friend – he does business with my husband.'

A rattle at the door announces the arrival of grand crèmes, along with doll-sized croissants and brioches.

Madeleine leans forward and fixes large green eyes on you as you sip. 'To create a perfume for a woman, it is necessary to first get to know her. Fragrance is such a deeply personal thing. My work makes me a combination of chemist, psychologist, magician, confessor. So, we shall spend some time today talking all about you.'

You probably look startled, because she laughs: 'There's no need for alarm. It will be painless, I promise. And there will be champagne, too. But let me begin by explaining the science . . .'

She starts to describe the chemistry that's at the heart of all those scents in duty-free shops and department stores, leading you out of the laboratory to show you some of the exhibits in the museum to illustrate her points. Time flies, and you have to admit, you're having fun.

At last, back in the quiet room full of perfume oils and pipettes, she extracts a bottle of champagne from a bar fridge and says, 'So, now you have some idea of the theory. But to make you an unforgettable perfume in the here and now, I need to know more about you.' She pours you each a glass of straw-coloured bubbles, then holds hers out to chink against yours. 'Here's to revelation,' she says. 'I wonder what mysteries you have locked up inside?'

'Oh,' you demur, flapping your hands. 'Nothing mysterious about me, just a regular girl ...'

'Well, to begin with, why don't you tell me how you come to be visiting Claudio in Venice? It's the strangest thing – he couldn't tell me anything about you.'

You slump. The last thing you want to do is tell this fabulously sophisticated woman about how you were tricked into flying to Venice by a randy octogenarian, but you sense she won't take no for an answer.

'Tell me what's troubling you. I have time, and we have champagne. The whole story, please, but no tears – they will block your nose and spoil the perfumes for you.'

It's actually a relief to get it all out, and when you're finished, Madeleine rises to her feet, almost triumphantly. 'But this is perfect!' she says.

You stare at her. 'What do you mean?'

'True, this is not a happy story – you were deceived. But this tells me all I need to know to make the perfect fragrance for you. You took a risk. You are impulsive. Passionate. You will go to the ends of the earth to give love a chance. In fact, I have the name for your perfume – we shall call it "Impetuous"!'

This woman should be a politician, given her ability to spin disaster. But you do feel a lot better all of a sudden. Maybe you won't be creeping home covered in humiliation after all. You'll be heading back with a unique perfume named 'Impetuous' in your honour.

You smile at Madeleine. 'I'm ready for the next step,' you say.

'Are you indeed,' she murmurs, leading you to a semi-circular desk – known as a perfume organ – its shelves filled with ranks of essential oils. There's a fan of paper tapers, and a jar of coffee beans. 'Choosing your oils can be overwhelming after a while,' Madeleine explains. 'So when you need a break, sniff at your coffee beans – it clears the nose. We begin with a carrier oil, something that feels good on the skin, and won't argue with any of the scents,' she continues, handing you a flask of almond oil. 'See how smoothly it goes on.' She dabs a tiny drop on to the back of your hand, and strokes it in, her slim fingers soothing.

Her hands fly deftly amongst the little bottles,

selecting some, rejecting others. She opens little containers with names like poetry – tonka bean, chypre, frankincense, clary sage and neroli, as well as some that make you think of gardens – rosewood, basil, mandarin, carnation, jasmine.

'Tell me what you like. What speaks to you?' she says, offering you the paper wands, and inviting you to dip them into the oils and smell them. The effect is heady – one concentrated fragrance after another, some so strong they're almost overwhelming.

'That's actually quite dark,' you say, as Madeleine extends a wand of oakmoss under your nose.

'Ah, it's all about the blend, the harmony between the oils. All fragrances need a top note, a middle note and a base note.'

She places her hands delicately on either side of your head: 'The top notes fly off the perfume first – they make the first impression, like someone's eyes or smile.' She circles her fingers slowly on your temples, and you can't help exhaling, relaxing back in your chair – a little pampering is just what you need.

'The middle notes last longer – they give roundness to the scent, warmth. They are sometimes called the heart notes, and with good reason.' As Madeleine speaks, she lays two cool fingers momentarily on the skin of your chest, just above your breast, and taps softly. 'They are the heartbeat of the fragrance.'

You don't know whether it's the powerful scents you've been inhaling, the release of telling your story or this woman's hands, but you find yourself shifting in your chair, and not with discomfort. You'd like her to stroke you a little more – as if you were a cat, you tell yourself.

As if she hears your thoughts, Madeleine says, 'And finally, there are the bottom notes, which last the longest. The darkest, but the ones that sustain, that keep the intrigue alive.' As she speaks, she drops her hands to your hips, cupping them very lightly. 'You see, it's from here that we draw our energy.'

There's a pause, as she stands bent over you, her hands still on your hips, her face alongside yours, so close you can hear her breathing and draw in her own subtle scent, something green with a dash of spice. Turning your head, you find yourself staring into her eyes, and you're conscious of her soft red mouth, only an inch from yours. You know you have only seconds in which to act, or the moment will be lost for ever. You also know any move – if you make a move at all – will have to come from you. But you've never done anything like this before.

But didn't Madeleine just call you 'impetuous', as if it was a badge of pride?

This is just not for you. It's easier to let the moment go past and focus on concocting your perfume. Go to page 201.

What the hell – you're going to live up to your 'impetuous' label. Go to page 193.

You take a deep breath, and then lean forward. It's a tiny distance, but somewhere in your mind, you hear Neil Armstrong's words, 'One giant leap for mankind' (or 'womankind' in your case) as your mouth brushes against Madeleine's. She doesn't kiss you back, but she doesn't draw away either, and her hands begin to slide up from your hips towards your waist in an unmistakable caress.

You kiss her again – her lips are incredibly soft and plump compared with those of the men you've been with: her upper lip is especially tender, and you suck gently at it. It's as if the world has shifted into slow motion, and it takes for ever for her tongue to slide against your lips, tap at your teeth, and then delve into your mouth. The sensation is intriguing, and you keep your eyes closed, also enjoying her hands – smaller than you're used to – as they creep slowly up your torso.

She's still bent over you, and without breaking the contact between your mouths, she coaxes you to your feet, and leads you in little steps over to the chaise longue in the corner, where you both sink down, and start kissing in earnest.

Then she utters a small exclamation, draws back from you and gets up. Oh no – did you do something wrong? But she's merely closing the blinds at the window, and also shedding her jacket. Underneath, she's wearing one of those all-in-one bustier undergarments that the French do so well, in delicate black lace. You're relieved that you put on one of your pretty new uplift bras that morning, and start unbuttoning your blouse with clumsy fingers.

'Here, let me,' Madeleine says, making short work of the job, folding your top and setting it aside. Then she takes a long look at you and lightly touches one of your nipples, already hard, through the fabric of your bra. 'So, are you sure you want to continue this ... exploration?' she asks. 'I can see this is new to you. But I think you are ... open to fresh experiences, yes?'

You hesitate, but only for a moment. You're in a foreign country, in a perfume laboratory with a sophisticated, sexy Frenchwoman – it's not like this opportunity will ever present itself again. Shouldn't you take advantage of the moment? 'Impetuous,' you mutter to yourself, and Madeleine hears you, and laughs, a low gurgle.

'I think I need to repeat my lesson about essential

oils,' she says, pressing you down on the chaise longue. She sits down next to you, and begins efficiently stripping off her shoes, suit skirt and satin knickers. You register that she's a natural red-head, her bush as neat as everything else about her.

Then she leans over you, dressed only in the bustier. 'First, the top notes – the head of the perfume, if you like ...' and she presses kisses all over your face and neck, nipping at your ears. You shudder as the little nibbles and nips rain down on your flushed skin, travelling slowly from your neck to your shoulders.

You feel her hands deftly undoing the hooks of your bra – it makes sense that a woman would be efficient about managing those – and then her voice, slightly throatier: 'Then there are the middle notes, the ones that give a scent body ...' You feel her warm breath travelling over your breasts, followed by a cupping hand. You groan quietly as her fingers tweak at your nipples, then more loudly as her mouth comes down on first one breast, then the other, lashing the nipples with her tongue. Her voice is muffled against your skin, but you hear her say, 'This is the heart of the fragrance.'

Partly out of hunger, partly out of curiosity, you

stretch your hands to her own small, startlingly pale breasts. They're spilling over the edge of her bustier, and you knead them, fascinated by the contrast between the incredible softness of her flesh and the stiffness of the lace.

'Wait, I haven't finished my lesson yet,' she says, sliding her hands down your ribcage, into the indentations of your waist, then down to your hips. 'Most important of all are the base notes: the ones that last longest, that give the scent its essence ...'

She strips off your panties almost briskly, then slides her hands far more languorously over the tops of your thighs, spreading her thumbs over your mound. You're speechless, but you open your legs in a silent invitation, and she slips a hand between your thighs.

'You could say that these deep notes form the core of the perfume.' At her words, she probes between your swollen lips, and you both gasp at the hot wetness she finds. She slides two fingers deep inside you before you have time to think about what's happening, and you arch like a bow and draw your legs up, astonished at the pleasure you're experiencing, at how much more you want.

'And this is at the core of every woman's personal

scent. This is what determines her essence,' Madeleine concludes. With that, she pushes your legs apart and up, and swoops down on your pussy with her mouth. Her lips and tongue on and between your crevices are sweet torture, and you thrash and cry out as she holds you down with strong but supple hands.

She flicks your clit with her tongue until you're whimpering and your hips are lifting, then draws away, teasing, to dart her tongue into the entrance to your pussy. And when that's too much to bear, she returns to your clit, trailing around it, pressing on it, fingers now as well as lips.

The blissful torment goes on for what feels like an aeon, but no matter how much she plays and teases and withdraws, your orgasm can't be denied – it's approaching like a runaway train – and it hits you with as much force, jack-knifing your body, forcing your hips right up off the chaise longue, your pussy pressing hard against Madeleine's mouth. It takes a while for you to realise that she's had to stretch a hand up over your mouth to muffle your hoarse screams.

As you lie twitching, release trickling through your veins like golden syrup, she straddles you, opening her legs wide. Her neat breasts have escaped the bustier, and her nipples are the same deep pink as her cunt, which she is opening to you with her fingers, spreading the engorged lips, showing you her own gleaming arousal.

You're not sure what she wants you to do, but it seems she has things in hand – she simply tilts her pelvis and grinds her pussy against yours, rubbing her clit against your wet folds, rocking and thrusting like a man. Within minutes, her head snaps back, her nipples darken, and she jerks again and again as she straddles you, crying out in short gasps.

At last she slumps down next to you and kisses you softly, and you taste yourself on her lips, and it causes another gentle wave of pleasure to wash through you.

You lie together in a comfortable silence, and then Madeleine gets to her feet, and moves to the perfume organ, where she collects several bottles and flasks.

'You relax,' she says. 'I need to finish mixing your perfume. And now I know exactly what to include.'

She rubs sweet almond oil on to your tummy, chest, breasts, arms and thighs, and then follows up with tiny drops of fragrance, smoothing the volatile oils into your skin.

'See, I am adding musk for boldness, ginger for warmth, lemon verbena for freshness and gardenia for sensuality. Do you like your new fragrance, Mademoiselle Impetuous?'

You like it very much. And you also like that her stroking hand is once again reaching between your thighs, anointing your clit with warm oil, circling slowly but powerfully around and across your sensitive nub. This time, you take longer to climb the heights, but eventually, your pelvis rocking, you cry out again as pleasure explodes in your pussy and radiates outwards.

For a long time after that, you're barely conscious. And for the next few hours, during the final preparation of your perfume, the recording of the formula so that it can be replicated whenever you need, and the choosing of the container before the mixture is sent away to mature, you can't stop smiling lazily. Now and again, you raise your arm to your nose to sniff at the blend of oils on your skin, made all the spicier for a dash of sex.

Over a lunch of warm goat's cheese salad and bouillabaisse served with more champagne, followed by lavender macaroons delivered in ribboned boxes, you remember something Madeleine said. 'I don't mean to pry or to offend, but I've never done anything like this before – I mean, with a woman – so I'm curious,' you begin. 'Didn't you mention a husband? Um, how does it work – are you gay? Or just, ah, flexible?'

Madeleine chuckles. 'I am very happily married with three beautiful children. My husband and I, we have a strong partnership. We also have an understanding. He has a mistress; and I have my ... adventures. Nobody is disappointed, everyone is discreet. Our children are raised in an atmosphere that is civil and contented.'

'Gosh,' you murmur. 'I'm not sure I could ever be that pragmatic.' But then you consider where your romantic streak has got you – deceived and stranded in a foreign country. On the other hand, you could also argue that it was indirectly responsible for getting you on to a chaise longue with an elegant and sexy perfumer. And you still have a ride home on a private plane with a handsome Italian Count ahead. So it's not all bad.

Go to page 201.

You're on the plane back to Venice with Claudio

You lean back in your seat as the coast of the South of France falls away against a romantic sunset haze, and sigh luxuriously.

Claudio looks up from his tablet: 'I hope your day was a success. Did Madeleine take proper care of you? She is a woman of many talents, that one.'

You shoot him a sharp look, but his remark seems innocent. 'You have no idea,' you say under your breath, and a little more loudly, 'I had a lovely time, thank you.' You're certainly not going to share all the day's surprises with him.

He lifts his head and sniffs appreciatively. 'I hope you don't mind me saying so, but you smell wonderful. Good enough to eat.'

That earns him another look, but you give him the benefit of the doubt, especially as he's smiling at you with real warmth – you realise you haven't really seen him smile before, and it transforms his face, adding dimples to his masculine chin.

'Thank you. I'm just wearing an approximate blend of oils for now – the actual perfume needs to mature for a few weeks. They'll send it on to me.'

'May I ask what name you chose for your personal perfume?'

You blush. 'You'll laugh – "Impetuous". It was Madeleine's idea,' you add hastily.

He does laugh, flashing perfect white teeth. 'It's a pity you won't be able to wear your new perfume to our opera evening. You are coming, I hope?'

You consider the prospect for a minute. You're not exactly an opera buff, and the idea of proper costumes and masks is a bit intimidating. But it also sounds like it could be a real adventure – you don't want to miss out.

'Thank you, I'd like that very much. If Adriana doesn't mind helping me find a costume and the rest of the stuff I'll need.'

'Excellent. She'll be happy to help – she enjoys that kind of thing.' He smiles again, and it makes your knees slightly fizzy. Perhaps you'll end up in a private opera box with him, all velvet curtains and plush chairs ... or dancing in his arms across a magnificent room under glittering chandeliers. A girl can dream, can't she?

Go to page 203.

You're getting ready for the opera

You gaze around the upmarket costume emporium in a tiny alley near La Fenice, the opera house, as Adriana and the proprietor, who appear to be old friends, chat about the evening ahead. Luxurious fabrics and outfits hang from every available inch of space, silks, satins and velvet gleaming dully in the muted Venetian light.

On the back wall of the shop, a flat-screen television plays highlights from the last *Carnevale*'s most glittering event, the Doge's Ball, and you're astounded at how lavish and inventive the costumes are. The guests are impeccably turned out, not a hair out of place, and everyone except for the musicians wears masks. Some of the women have masks that cover only their eyes, but the men are either wearing half-masks that cover the entire face except for the mouth or full-face masks, often in gold. The effect is slightly sinister, slightly decadent and definitely glamorous.

Adriana and her friend have an armful of costumes for you to try, and you step into a tiny dressing room and strip to your undies. They keep pulling magnificent creations over your head and lacing you into them – it's like a history lesson as you try on gowns representing four different centuries, each one more opulent than the last.

The trouble is, they're all heavy, involving yards of fabric and complicated petticoats, panniers, crinolines and corsets. You admire yourself in one lemon-coloured outfit – the boned bodice squeezes your breasts upwards, giving you the most magnificent cleavage – but you can barely breathe, and certainly can't imagine sitting still through an entire opera in it, much less eating or drinking.

'I'm so sorry, this isn't working for me,' you say at last, surrounded by piles of brocade and silk. 'Is it a rule that the costume has to be historical? Or am I allowed to wear something else?'

Adriana clicks her fingers. 'I have an idea – what about the dancers' costumes?' She dives into another rack of clothing, but then you spot the outfit of your dreams hung high on the wall – a closely fitted bodice of what looks like peacock feathers curling up over one shoulder, and a filmy blue skirt made of layers of tulle, ballet length.

The others follow your gaze: 'Ah yes, I made that for the lead dancer in one of our recent ballets at La

Fenice,' says the proprietor. 'It is indeed exquisite, and it looks as if it might fit – I used lacing at the back so that it can expand to accommodate more than one size.'

She gets it down and hands it to you – it really is made from peacock feathers, carefully applied to a violet satin bodice and anchored in place by sequins, crystals and seed pearls. You pray it fits – it's the most romantic dress you've ever laid eyes on.

Adriana lets the laces out and helps you into it, and it settles over you like a second skin. You look in the mirror, and it's as if a fairy godmother has waved a wand: you've never looked so glamorous in your life.

The two women confer: 'She will have to wear it without a brassiere, because of the open lacing at the back. And what shall we do about shoes?'

Half an hour later, you walk out slightly dazed. You've been outfitted not just with the dress, but with a gauzy silver shawl, a faux-pearl choker with matching earrings, pale stockings and suspender belt, the all-important mask and a pair of turquoise ballet-style flats. You considered heels for a minute, but even a short stay in Venice has taught you that it's a city of uneven stones, puddles, slippery marble, steps and bridges.

You feel faint at the thought of the bill, but Adriana seemed unconcerned: 'We have an account here,' was all she said when you tried to raise the matter. 'Come to our palazzo later this afternoon,' she instructs. 'Have a little siesta first – it's going to be a late night. The hairdresser will be coming at six – she will also do our makeup,' she adds. 'And after that, gondolas will take us to the opera venue.'

Now dusk is stealing in, and you feel exactly like Cinderella. After a luxurious nap and a soak in your bathtub – rapidly becoming your favourite place in Venice – you've been at the Palazzo Grania for the last hour, being primped within an inch of your life. You and Adriana are ready at last, and you check yourself in the eighteenth-century gilt mirror one more time.

Maybe it's the soft patina of the old looking-glass, but you barely recognise yourself. The hairdresser styled your hair so that your nape is bare, making your neck look much longer, and your shoulders, polished with one of those glittery body lotions, rise out of the soft feathers of the bodice.

Adriana is wearing a Renaissance dress in gold and

blue brocade, as well as a small fortune's worth of jewellery, and her hair has been piled elaborately on her head. You both pick up your masks – hers is a traditional black and white half-mask, but yours is a lighter concoction of feathers that covers only your eyes – and head out to meet the men.

Claudio and his father are waiting for you at the foot of the staircase, both simply but elegantly dressed in white frilled shirts and period breeches and boots, topped with magnificent full-length black cloaks.

The jaws of both men drop as you emerge, and you descend the stairs, feeling very self-conscious in your finery. It doesn't help that Claudio Senior whoops and applauds, although you like the fact that his son is openly staring at you.

Mr Silent – also dressed in the identical costume – comes in to inform you that the gondolas are ready. He stops mid-sentence as he catches sight of you, and there's an intense and approving silence as he stares at you.

As you're leaving the building, Van rushes in, still in jeans. 'Sorry I'm late, everyone – wow!' He stops to whistle at you and Adriana: 'Ladies, you look absolutely sensational! Listen, go ahead without me.

I'll get a water-taxi and catch up with you at the opera. Save a seat for me!' This is addressed to you, with a wink.

He disappears, and the three remaining men all don black tricorn hats and masks that cover their entire faces apart from their mouths – they look like very handsome highwaymen. Then you're being handed into one of the gondolas, and there's a rather undignified scramble as Claudio's father tries to sit next to you, and is thwarted by his son. You're just relieved no one ends up in the drink, and lean back against the padded red seat, which gives you a duck's-eye view of the canal and the palazzos dreaming on either side of it.

A few other members of the opera party have joined you for the gondola trip, and as your small flotilla sets off, the gondoliers punting their crafts along in a distinctive gliding motion, a bear of a man in the prow of one of the boats breaks into song, belting out a popular opera aria in a deep baritone.

Anywhere else, it would be completely over-the-top, but here it's taken as natural, and you're entranced. 'I thought the gondoliers did the singing?' you ask Claudio, and he explains that this is a common misconception – it's more usual to hire professional musicians to do the serenading.

All too soon, you're drawing up at a palazzo with so much delicate marble carving on its façade, it looks like a piece of starched lace. By now, you've grown accustomed to hopping on to slightly swaying pontoons and docks, and you manage to swan into the building as if you've been arriving by boat all your life.

Inside, it's a blur of chandeliers, pillars and tapestries, and a small crowd of immaculately attired people chatting in a combination of different languages against the strains of a string quartet. You blink – aren't those some of the younger Grimaldis in that corner? It's impossible to tell for sure, though, as almost everyone is in masks, but there is a great deal of air-kissing and laughter nonetheless, while waiters in full eighteenth-century regalia are handing round glasses of Prosecco and melt-in-the-mouth canapés.

Then someone claps their hands, and you all troop through to a long drawing room in which chairs have been set out, and take your seats in front of a dais. The conductor leads in the small orchestra, his violin tucked under his arm, and after applause, the overture to *La Traviata* begins.

Sitting between the two Claudios, who have supplied you with an embossed programme, you soon lose yourself in the music. It's very different when opera is up close and personal like this – the singers are only feet away – and slightly to your surprise, you're really enjoying it.

However, there's a snake in this paradise: halfway through the first act, the older man's hand descends on to your thigh. You peel it off and toss it back in his direction, but he clearly thinks you're playing some sort of game – within minutes, his hand is back.

'Please stop it!' you hiss at him, but the only response is a lascivious smile – all you can see of his face under the mask – as his hand climbs even higher. Oh bugger. By dint of much leg-crossing and twitching, you manage to get to the end of the first act relatively unscathed, but by the time the singers bow and troop off the dais, you realise you need back-up.

'I'm so sorry,' you whisper in the younger Claudio's ear, 'but I need to change seats with you. Er, your father …'

Fortunately, he gets the message immediately, glares at his father, and murmurs, 'No need to worry.' You all proceed into another, even more dazzling room for the second act and, at the last minute, you and Claudio swap seats.

That's better. You start to relax, giving yourself over to the magic of the experience – your fairy-tale frock, the room full of masked strangers, the Prosecco fizzing in your veins, the romantic and vaguely familiar arias. And are you imagining things, or is Claudio's leg pressing up against yours? You slide a touch closer to him, and he doesn't shift away. And now a hand is caressing your shoulder ... a very good sign, until you realise that both of Claudio's hands are neatly folded in his lap. Oh no. Claudio Senior has reached a hand across behind his son, and is happily giving you a good feel. Now what?

Desperate times call for desperate measures, you decide, and after shrugging off the leech, you snuggle up to Claudio, pressing yourself against his body. He throws you a startled glance, then correctly assesses the situation, and puts an arm around your shoulders, acting as a human barrier. His hand is warm and dry on your bare skin, and you give a little shiver.

All too soon, the act comes to an end, and everyone gets up to circulate and sip more Prosecco. You wander off to examine a painting of a Renaissance

Madonna, and when you look up, the room is emptying again.

But Claudio is at the door, an imposing sight in his cloak and highwayman's hat, beckoning you to follow him. Instead of leading you back to the opera, however, he heads down a shadowy passage. You scamper after him, a little puzzled, but he stops to let you catch up, and to your delight, presses a quick and scalding kiss on your mouth.

Then he strides off again, his cloak swirling around his legs. You reach for his hand, halting him, and this time you're the one who kisses him, hungry for that voluptuously shaped mouth. He holds you at arm's length, looking down at you, his eyes gleaming through the holes in the mask. Then he nods as if satisfied, presses your hand to his lips in a courtly gesture – and leads you through the grand mansion, down stairs and through what looks like a secret tunnel, your fingers interlocked the whole way.

The next moment, you're out in the night air, alongside a quiet canal. Claudio keeps going, and you follow. You're glad you settled for ballet slippers – you'd break your neck in heels, the pace you're going. Around a corner, you come to an archway that leads to a dead end – another canal. It's dimly lit by one of those old-world streetlights seen throughout Venice. Claudio leads you under the arch, then pulls you against his body.

You're flattered to feel a substantial erection pressing against you – who knew you were having such an effect on him? Your masks and costumes, the setting – both daringly outdoor and intimately private – all go to your head, and you melt in his arms, dizzy, tilting your pelvis up against him invitingly. He delves into the bodice of your dress, and you murmur to him to be careful of the delicate feathers – and then gasp as he lifts your breasts out, exposing them. The night air isn't exactly cold, but it's slightly clammy, and curls of mist are rising up from the water.

Claudio's hands are warm and caressing, though, and you lean back a little and flaunt yourself at him, relishing his hands cupping and clasping, tracing paths over your nipples, now hard and pointed.

You run your hands from his shoulders down his chest, taking your time as you explore the muscles under the fine fabric. And then you boldly put the flat of one hand against his crotch, and he makes a noise deep in his throat, and swoops down on your mouth again. His mask is smooth and chilly against your face, his lips and tongue delectably warm and alive by contrast.

As you kiss, Claudio chivalrously enfolds you in his cloak, pulling the edges around you. Once you're safely cocooned, he picks you up and swings you round until your feet find a little ledge – which puts your groin at the same level as his. His cloak is warm and smells of his cologne, and it also forms a barrier between your skin (and even more vital, your dress) and the old stone wall of the archway.

'Is this your invisibility cloak?' you ask, and to your surprise he snorts with laughter – you'd never have picked Claudio as a Harry Potter buff.

Meanwhile, his hand is fighting its way through the layers of tulle that make up your skirt. You both catch your breath as he finds your stockings and suspenders, and the tender stretch of thigh between the two.

He whispers, 'Are you sure?' and something about his voice – the accent – rings a faraway bell. You hesitate, then seize the edge of his mask, and push it up, revealing his face.

Oh dear God. It's Van! You reel back in shock. 'What are you doing here?' you shriek in a strangled voice.

'I'm having a fantastic time with you, as if it wasn't blindingly obvious,' he says, bewildered. 'What's the problem?'

'I thought you were your brother!' you wail, clutching your head.

'What? You're joking! You mean—' He looks as horrified as you feel.

'I'm so sorry – but you're wearing the same costumes and masks! How was I to know?'

'*Fuck*.' Van swears a blue streak, and you don't blame him. 'I don't believe this,' he says. 'And here I thought my charms had won you over.'

What are you going to do now? Van is incredibly sexy, and you're so aroused, you're not sure you want to stop. But what about Claudio? You can't change gears just like that! Or can you?

To go *ahead and finish what you started with Van*, go to page 216.
To *bail out and head back to the opera*, go to page 224.

215

Van's face is shadowed, so you can't tell what he's thinking, but even the most robust ego would be a bit bruised in a situation like this – being mistaken for another man, much less a rich, handsome older brother.

'Van,' you whisper, 'I'm sorry – it was Claudio I came to Venice to see – or thought I was coming to see, anyway. But you know what? The guy who's been kissing and touching me, wanting me, making me feel good – that's you. And I want you too.'

You lean forward and kiss him again, your naked breasts pressing against his chest, and after a moment's hesitation, his mouth moves against yours once more.

This time the kiss is greedy, and you respond in kind. You desperately want this man, right here, right now, and you fumble at his pants, not exactly familiar with the fastenings of period garments.

He laughs at your frantic efforts, guides your hand to his eager cock, and helps you to release it from his clothing. It pulses in your grasp, hot, velvety, and so hard you can feel the main vein threading over its surface.

You're suddenly worried about protection – it never

occurred to you that your accessories for the evening needed to include a condom – but miraculously, Van has conjured one from somewhere under his cloak. He clenches it between his teeth, and you both reach for the lace g-string you're wearing, tugging it down to leave you audaciously bare.

You lean back in his arms, *sans* knickers, your breasts bouncing free of your bodice, and your delicate skirt now above your waist. But you're shielded by his cloak, so you lift one leg and hook it around him, uncharacteristically bold.

He responds to your invitation by placing his hand high between your legs, a tantalising inch away from your pussy, and you feel yourself gush with anticipation. And then his fingers creep upwards, first one, then two, pushing firmly up into the warm swamp between your legs.

'God, you're wet,' he mumbles through the condom, still between his teeth. 'Feels fantastic.'

'Don't make me beg,' you respond, grabbing the little foil square, opening it, then rolling the condom carefully on to his cock. 'Right, we're good to go,' you murmur, hooking your leg higher around his hip, hungry for his huge erection.

He doesn't disappoint – his cock is immediately pressing against you, eager for access, the head teasing at the entrance to your pussy. It takes you a few seconds of tilting and adjusting, his hands cupping your bottom, and then he starts sliding in and up, slowly at first, and then all the way in with one powerful thrust.

His cock feels so good, and you tell him that as he starts to move inside you, rocking at first, then pressing harder and deeper, lifting you off the ground with each movement of his pelvis.

You're not used to stand-up sex, and it feels strange, but in a good way – you have to hang on to Van to keep your balance, abandoning yourself to him, especially as his thrusts grow more powerful. You can't help crying out in time with his rhythmic movements, and you're aching for an orgasm, but you're not sure you can relax enough in this position.

As if reading your mind, Van reaches down, his hands squeezing the tender skin of your buttocks, then grasping them and lifting you up slightly. Now you wrap both legs around his waist, sling your arms around his neck, and lean back against the wall, the thick fabric of the cloak acting as a buffer. Van's hands support you as you're pinned on the fulcrum of his erection, and you give yourself over entirely to the sensation of his thrusts as they get deeper and faster. You're dimly aware that the sounds you're making are both amplified by the arch and muffled by the nearby water, and it adds to the dreamlike quality of the experience.

You feel ripples building, and you pray he holds on, and then the first waves pulse through you, and your pussy clenches again and again as you come, convulsing against him, feeling the release wash through you as you cry out, the noise muffled against his neck. And then you cling on with nerveless arms and pray he doesn't drop you as he heaves inside you, shouting out with the force of his own release.

After a long moment when the earth apparently stops spinning on its axis, you unfold yourself from Van's grip and slide towards the ground like limp spaghetti. Fortunately, he hangs on to you.

'Wow,' you say, and he echoes you: 'Wow indeed.'

You spend a few minutes rearranging your clothing, checking that your earrings are still in place and smoothing down your hair – you're sure you have lipstick everywhere, as it's smeared all over Van's face, along with a trace of the glitter the makeup artist used on your eyes. You giggle as you use the corner of his cloak to try to tidy him up.

At last you're both looking a little more respectable. 'Time we went back to the others, I think,' you say. 'We don't want anyone sending out a search party.'

He looks at you with his head on one side. 'Opera's not really my thing. Listen, this has been really great. What do you say we split town? Tomorrow I'm heading to Zermatt for some skiing. I'm joining some mates who've got a chalet there – everything you need for fun, a big fireplace and a hot tub. Wanna come along for the ride?'

You didn't see that one coming – now what? Do you drop everything and head off with Van? You're certainly tempted, especially after the magical encounter you've just had. But you barely know this guy – maybe he's too wild for you. And how would you explain to Claudio? Perhaps you should stay right here – who knows what Venice still has to offer?

To *head off to fresh pastures with Van*, go to page 221.
To *walk away from Van*, go to page 223.

You've decided to head off with Van

You take a long look at Van, trying to see past the bravado, the playboy act. The faint sprinkling of freckles across his nose makes you imagine him as a child. You picture the lonely boy he must have been, a jet-setting mother and philandering father packing him off to boarding-schools in another country. No wonder he became such a party animal – it must have been either that or retreating into a shell of isolation.

He grins at you hopefully, and Venice suddenly feels too formal, too melancholy, a beautiful otherworldly place always looking back to the past. And it's not as if you owe Claudio any explanations, given that your online relationship with him turned out to be a mirage.

You reach out and take Van's hand. The prospect of a few days of fun with him, along with snow and sparkling air – and yes, a hot tub for intimate evenings – is growing on you. You have no illusions about a future with him, but who knows what might happen? At the very least, you're going to have some amazing stories to tell your grandchildren. Once they're over eighteen, that is.

You smile up into his grey eyes. 'Hmm. Will there be hot chocolate?'

'There will definitely be hot chocolate. In fact, I think I can promise you whipped cream, too. In interesting places.'

'You're on,' you say. 'Zermatt it is. Now come back to the hotel with me – I'll need help packing.'

His face cracks into the broadest smile, and as he bends to kiss you again, it occurs to you that maybe – just maybe – you've ended up with the right Lazzari man after all.

THE END

You've decided to walk away from Van

You gaze up at Van's face, and something about his smile, so confident – over-confident, in fact – grates on you. He's just too cocky – literally. 'That hot tub you mentioned? You were thinking of just the two of us, weren't you?'

'Hell, no! That place is Orgy Central – such a blast. I have to admit, I can't wait to watch you and Rowena getting it on. Or wait, you and Tiffany ...'

'You won't be watching me with anyone, Van. It's been sweet, but it's over. I'll be quite happy on my own from here.' And with that, you head back to the palazzo. Maybe you'll be in time to catch the last aria.

Go to page 224.

Back in the palazzo, you manage to negotiate the maze of passages through the ancient building, following the sound of music. On the way you nip into a palatial bathroom (how much marble can there be in one small city? No wonder it's sinking into the sea) to do running repairs to your makeup.

Once you're presentable, you tiptoe back into the room, where a soprano is dying in the arms of her beloved, a fate that is in no way interfering with her ability to sing at the top of her voice.

You wait until she expires in a crescendo of notes, followed by a storm of applause and cries of '*Brava!*' Then you run over to Claudio, who is getting to his feet and looking around. You peer at him closely: 'Claudio – that *is* you, isn't it?'

The eyes looking back at you through the mask are definitely dark brown. 'Of course it's me,' he says. 'Where did you disappear to? I was a little worried.'

'Oh – er, I wandered off to explore and got a little … waylaid. No worries, though, I'm here now.'

He tucks your arm under his, and leads you off to where the waiters are circulating with yet more delectable titbits. A string quartet is now playing a medley of better-known tunes from the opera, and a few couples are even waltzing.

'May I say how lovely you look tonight?' he says formally.

'Right back at you,' you reply, and when he looks puzzled, you add, 'Thank you – I had help. Are you sure Adriana wasn't a fairy godmother in a previous life? I'm so grateful to her, and to you, for all you're doing for me. Tonight was … extraordinary. What happens now?'

'What happens now is that I ask you if you would do me the honour of accompanying me to dinner tomorrow night. It would be good to get to know you a little better, especially after what you've gone through at the hands of my family.'

You splutter into your glass. Crikey, if only he knew. You try not to think of Van's hands, and where they've just been.

'Are you all right?' asks Claudio, still solicitous.

'Yes, yes, of course. Just a sip that went down the wrong way.' You give your best brilliant smile. 'Dinner would be lovely, thank you.'

'Excellent. If there's anywhere you would like to go

especially, let Adriana know so she can make the booking. Otherwise I shall meet you at the hotel at eight. They have an excellent menu. I can recommend the risotto with vodka and scallops.'

The remainder of the evening passes in a haze of champagne, music and shimmering lights. As your head sinks on to your pillow that night, you're too tired even to dream. But in the seconds before you fall asleep, you acknowledge that you're pretty excited about tomorrow's dinner. At last, some quality time alone with Claudio – perhaps there's a chance of a fairy-tale ending after all.

Go to page 227.

At last. It's been a perfect evening, after a perfect day. You spent the afternoon at the hotel spa, getting the full works – facial, manicure and pedicure. Dinner has been like something out of an old black-and-white movie, right down to the pianist tinkling out jazz classics in the corner. Claudio has been the perfect companion, witty and charming. He's been modest about reading History at Cambridge, and his MBA from one of Europe's top business schools. He's asked all about you, your family, friends and career. Best of all, he keeps smiling at you. And every time he does, butterflies swirl and swoop in your tummy.

Emboldened by the fragrant rosé wine you've been drinking, you ask why he's so interested in your life. After all, it couldn't be more different from his.

He lifts one shoulder. 'I know I have no business complaining, but the circles I move in are so small – remnants of European aristocracy, with a sprinkling of new money – the oligarchs from Russia and elsewhere. And they are the same, year in, year out. The same faces, the same gossip, the same society weddings, designer outfits. It's reached the stage where the women in particular are starting to blur together for me. They're all too thin, and too tanned, and it's frightening how they don't age. They seem to ...' – he pauses and pinches the air with his fingers – 'desiccate instead. You're such a breath of fresh air by comparison.'

As you swallow your last mouthful of panna cotta with chestnut sauce, the hovering waiter offers liqueurs. You look at Claudio across the table: you can't be imagining the spark in his eyes. You take a deep breath: 'Shall we go up to my suite for an after-dinner drink?'

'I would be delighted,' he says, getting to his feet with alacrity and pulling out your chair for you. You walk sedately to the tiny lift, even though the butter-flies are now looping the loop, but once you're in, he whispers in your ear: 'I thought you'd never ask!'

His mouth is inches from yours, the beautiful mouth that's featured in so many fantasies, that you've imagined kissing for so long. You're trembling with desire, and lift your face to his almost helplessly, your lips opening. Every cell in your body is saying *please please please*, and he's moving closer, so close you can feel the heat radiating off his skin – and then the lift judders to a stop and the door slides open. '*Buona sera!*' chirps the little old lady waiting to enter the lift, and you sidle out past her, smiling through clenched teeth.

You grab Claudio's hand, and by the time you reach your room, you're shamelessly dragging the man. You tumble through the door, and at last you're kissing hot and hard, almost devouring each other, tongues searching and plunging, teeth clashing, tearing at each other's clothes. To your delight, Claudio has turned from a smooth cosmopolitan man of manners into an animal – he all but pushes you towards the bed and starts fighting his way out of his tailored garments, still kissing you, ravaging your face and neck, nipping at your shoulders.

At last he's left in only a pair of snow-white underpants, and you're in your favourite lingerie set – a bra with cunning uplift that gives you the cleavage of a canyon, and matching thong, all in ivory silk with embossed details.

You pirouette for him, and as he reaches for you, you back away, teasing. 'Not so fast ... all good things come to those who wait.' You sway your hips and reach behind you to unhook your bra, slowly sliding the straps off your shoulders, bumping and grinding as you let it peel away and fall to the floor. He growls and grabs at you, and you giggle and race round the bed.

'And for my next act ...' You start to ease off your teeny panties, still turning, flaunting yourself at him. It's too much for Claudio – he launches himself at you.

The sex isn't exactly what you expected. Go to page 231.

The sex is everything you've ever dreamed of. Go to page 239.

The sex isn't exactly how you imagined it would be

Claudio has you on the bed, naked except for the killer heels you put on especially for the evening, and judging from the hunger with which he's kissing you and squeezing your breasts, the sex you've imagined for so long is about to happen. You're on fire everywhere he touches you, and some places he hasn't.

'Claudio,' you gasp. 'My handbag. You'll find a condom in the inside pocket.'

He pulls back and peers at you. What – is he *pouting*? 'I assumed you'd have all that, er, under control? The Pill or something?' he asks.

You stare at him from your position flat on your back, incredulous. Surely he doesn't expect you to explain? What century is the guy living in, anyway?

Something about your expression conveys the message, and he huffs, 'Okay, okay, I'll fetch it.' While he fishes in your handbag and deals with the condom, you try to recapture the mood. 'Need a little help?' you purr.

'No, no, it's fine.' And then he smiles that melting-warm-chocolate smile, and the butterflies all break loose again, and you kiss passionately as he parts your legs and kneels between them.

He's in a hurry, but that's fine – so are you – and you almost sob with pleasure as you feel his cock pressing up against you, then into you, filling you up. You wind your arms around his neck, murmuring his name, giving yourself over to the feel of his thrusts – which are coming faster and faster, too fast, you can't catch his rhythm – and then, with a grunt and a grimace, he comes.

As he slumps on top of you as if shot, you're left with that sense of an orgasm all dressed up with no place to go, and your pussy throbs, but with disappointment, not satisfaction. Okay, you scold yourself, so the sex was all over in two minutes, but that was just the first round. The night is still young.

Eventually, once Claudio's breathing starts returning to normal, you pluck at his shoulder, and he gets the hint and rolls off you. 'My turn now,' you say coyly, and he responds with a non-committal grunt.

'Um, Claudio?' you press. 'What about me? Here's a hint,' and with that, you take his hand and draw it down to your bush.

He frowns down at you. 'What are you doing? Wait, are you saying I didn't satisfy you?'

You're absolutely floored. 'Excuse me, but I

assumed that sex would mean equal-opportunity orgasms.'

'What?' He stares at you uncomprehendingly.

'Pleasure *is* supposed to be shared, you know. Something your brother seems to understand—'

'My brother? You and *Van*?'

Oops. You didn't mean to let that slip out. Claudio looks as if he's about to have an apoplectic fit. 'You certainly move fast, you deceitful—'

'It wasn't like that! It was an accident – I swear I thought he was you!'

'An *accident*? I don't believe this – you're using that mistaken identity excuse again? Are you on a mission to work your way through my entire family?'

At this point, the two of you are at opposite ends of the bed, and you're clutching a pillow to hide your nakedness. Any desire you were feeling has evaporated. This man is not who you thought he was, and you just want him gone so you can raid the minibar. You know you saw your good friends Cadbury and Pringles in there.

Fortunately, the feeling seems mutual – you've never seen a man dress so fast. As he shoots his cuffs, his face softens a little. 'I apologise. That last remark was uncalled for and unfair. But the truth is, we don't know each other. And it seems we have made certain assumptions about each other.'

You nod, your anger ebbing away. He's right – you projected so much onto him, you turned him into Prince Charming in your head. Whereas he's a rather traditional businessman weighed down by too many responsibilities – and, frankly, not that great in the sack. And, you think wryly, when a guy is that rich and good-looking, not many women are going to risk a little hands-on training. The women he takes to bed probably only ever fawn and flatter.

'Claudio, perhaps this should be goodbye. I've had an unforgettable few days, and I'll always be grateful for that. But this isn't my world.'

'I think you're right. The suite is of course yours until the end of the week. Anything you need, just ask, and the hotel will arrange it for you.' He holds out his hand formally, and you realise he expects you to shake it.

Still clutching the pillow against you, you stick out a hand. 'Say goodbye and thank you to Adriana for me.'

And then he's gone, and with him, the last remnants of your Venetian dream. You heave a huge sigh. At least you gave it a shot. Then again … you do have the option of staying here for a few more days – it would be a shame to waste it. So what if it didn't work out with Claudio? Why can't you enjoy Venice on your own? Somewhat cheered, you pad into the bathroom to run yet another bubble bath, taking a giant slab of chocolate with you.

You're awoken by a soft tap on the door. It's early, not even eight a.m. You pull on your robe and peer through the peephole, taken aback when you see Mr Silent standing in the corridor. Has Claudio changed his mind about letting you use the business suite?

You open the door with some trepidation. 'Yes?'

'*Signorina*. May I come in?'

You sigh and wave him in. 'I know why you're here.'

He looks momentarily befuddled. 'You do?'

'Yes. Claudio's sent you to throw me out, hasn't he? Don't worry, I'm happy to go.'

'No. That is not it at all. I merely came to enquire if there was anything you needed.'

'Really?'

He smiles, which instantly turns his face from

inscrutable to warm and open. 'Truly. I know that things did not work out for you with the Lazzaris.'

That's putting it mildly. You sit down on the bed. What are you doing here, anyway? Were you really going to stay here and let the Lazzaris fund your holiday? Suddenly, all you want to do is get out of here. 'You know, I think it's time I left.'

'Leave Venice?' He looks genuinely disconcerted.

'Maybe. Either that or I'll have to find another hotel.'

'With the Biennale, it will not be easy.' He smiles again. 'But I have another option. Come, pack your things.'

'Where are we going?'

'You will see.'

You throw your clothes into the baby elephant's belly, leaving the opera costume laid out on the bed with a note for Adriana. You glance at it before you close the door, amazed that you don't feel a jot of regret.

You're expecting to head for the canal and a water-taxi, but instead Mr Silent takes your suitcase, and leads you through cobbled alleyways, past churches with medieval wells outside, children playing in courtyards and elderly men smoking outside neighbourhood bars. Eventually, he pauses outside a latticed door in a faded red wall, balconies overhead adorned with pots of petunias and strung with lines of washing.

He knocks on the door, and a rotund, elderly woman opens it, grins broadly and throws her arms around him.

'Damiano!' she says, kissing him all over his face.

He laughs at your expression. 'Meet my mother.' The woman immediately embraces you and plants two kisses on your cheeks.

You're drawn into a dark, cool entrance hall, and up a flight of stairs to a tiny room with an old-fashioned iron bed covered in starched white linen, a cross on the wall, and an antique desk made of heavy black wood. Everything smells of beeswax polish, and somewhere in the background, there's a whiff of sage and garlic frying.

'Here's your room. It's not very grand, but we will do whatever we can to make you comfortable. Mama doesn't speak much English, but I have a feeling you're going to get on very well.'

You feel instantly at home in this tranquil little

room, the simplicity of the décor broken only by small, vividly coloured abstracts on the wall. 'These are nice,' you say, pointing to one, and this leads to much beaming and a flood of Italian from Mr Silent's mother. He looks a touch sheepish: 'They're mine.'

The homeliness of your new surroundings comes almost as a respite after the grandeur of the hotel and the various palazzos you've visited, and you exhale.

'I must be getting back to work,' Damiano says.

You realise you wish he could stay, and are about to say so, when he says, 'Perhaps we could have dinner this evening? It will not be what you have become accustomed to, but ...'

'That would be lovely.'

With another of those warming smiles, he leaves.

You sit down on the bed. Perhaps Mr Silent is who you've been waiting for all along. Perhaps he isn't. But you're not about to rush to find out. You pull on a pair of comfortable shoes and smile to yourself. In the meantime, you've got your own love affair with the city to continue.

THE END

The sex is everything you've ever dreamed of

You tumble backwards on to the edge of the bed, and Claudio leans over you, trapping you between muscled arms. 'I can't resist you,' he murmurs, kissing you more lingeringly, his tongue sweeping around your mouth. You're going to have spectacular stubble rash tomorrow.

He strokes your hair and face, nibbles at your ears in turn, then trails his mouth up and down your neck, driving you wild with hunger. Then, tantalisingly slowly, he kisses his way down your shoulders. You moan and plead, and at last his tongue finds first one nipple, then the other, alternately licking and sucking, his hands holding your breasts steady for his mouth as you writhe beneath him.

Then he's pulling away, and you make a little noise of complaint that turns into another moan as his hand strokes the tiny piece of fabric, soaked through, that's shielding your pussy. Keeping that teasing hand between your legs, he steps out of his own underwear, revealing a thick, dark cock jutting out of a lustrous black bush. Then it's your turn, and he takes his time pulling your thong off as you rock your hips up to help.

'Open your legs for me,' he whispers. You're so helpless with lust that you pull your knees right up, then let them fall open, exposing yourself completely. 'Beautiful,' he murmurs, reapplying his fingers to the folds and crevices of your pussy lips.

'I can't stand it,' you manage to get out. 'Please – there's a condom in the inside pocket of my bag – please fuck me now.'

Claudio rolls the condom on to his erection in no time, then braces himself between your legs, standing between them, slightly lifting your bottom, still on the edge of the bed, towards him. It creates a fantastic angle of contact as the head of his cock settles at the entrance to your pussy. He circles his hips for a few minutes, teasing, making you thrash and beg for him, then he rams himself home with one smooth, deep thrust.

As you gasp at the girth of his cock, wider than you're used to, he scoops up your thighs, and drapes your legs, still shod in delicate silver high-heeled sandals, over his shoulders, rolling your pelvis right back, and enabling him to slide in an inch further. You don't think you've ever had someone this deep in your pussy before, and it's delirious. You throw your arms out in abandon, and give yourself over entirely to the growing storm of pleasure in your cunt. Claudio's movements are slow but sure and deep, and your pussy starts to ripple, then clutch, then spasm – and then you explode, coming again and again. Every time the waves die down, Claudio thrusts again, and you arch and cry out one more time, until he also roars and ejaculates, his firm buttocks heaving.

Much later, he takes off your shoes and kisses the arches of your feet, sucking your toes (thank goodness you had that pedicure). Then his mouth begins a leisurely journey all the way up one leg, and the entire blissful cycle begins again. Even later, you drift off in his arms, both of you completely sated.

Until the next morning, when you take a romantic bubble bath together. You knew that bathtub was big enough for two – but even so, there's quite a bit of water on the floor by the time you're finished, and you both smell as if you've been rolling in a rose garden.

Eventually you dress – you're both starving – and head up to the rooftop terrace where breakfast is served. The view of the silvery basin of San Marco, the serene edifice of the church on the island of San

Giorgio Maggiore across the lagoon, the most perfect eggs Benedict ever, and your very own Prince Charming smiling across the table at you – it just doesn't get better than this.

The idyllic mood is broken by the buzzing of Claudio's phone. He looks at the display and grimaces. 'I am so sorry, but I am afraid I have to take this.'

He snaps '*Pronto*,' into the phone, then, 'I'm busy. It will have to wait.' The voice on the other end won't take no for an answer, though, and Claudio, now conversing in rapid-fire Italian, grows increasingly curt.

Eventually he ends the call and sighs. 'I must apologise again. Some of the clients I saw in Nice have arrived to sort out a few details, and they insist on seeing me now. If I could decline, I would, but they say they cannot wait. I hope you don't mind if they join us?'

Oh well. It's not exactly how you hoped the morning would pan out, but you're so satisfied, you're feeling generous, and you wave your hand: 'No problem!'

A few minutes later, Mr Silent escorts in a troop of slab-faced businessmen. They draw up chairs at your table, and you don't like the way they look straight through you – although you like it even less when one gent with a bristle haircut and cold pale eyes stares openly at your breasts. The conversation that ensues is in French, although some of the guys talk to each other in Russian, if you're not mistaken.

Mr Silent doesn't sit down with the rest, but stands back against a wall, rocking very slightly on the balls of his feet. At some point, his phone chirps, and he reaches into his jacket for it – hang on, is that the strap of a holster? The penny drops – he's not the butler, he's Claudio's bodyguard.

Suddenly it's all too rich for your blood. You've had a glorious time, but you feel a pang for your simpler life back home, where the pictures on your walls are charity-shop finds or prints with personal meaning, where you don't have to worry about breaking the priceless china every time you have a cup of tea, where you're respected for working hard at your career, not for your lineage or wealth or looks. Plus you're unlikely to find yourself breakfasting with the Russian Mafia. This just isn't your world.

You get to your feet and cast Claudio a regretful smile. '*Grazie mille*,' you say in your best Italian, following it up with '*Arrivederci*.' And then you saunter out. You have a plane to catch – or you soon will have. You rather like the idea of going home and regaling your friends with your adventures.

And then you realise, going home isn't the only option open to you … you've come this far, why not throw the dice again, and head for Amsterdam – or even Manhattan? You've still got a bit of leave due to you, and thanks to the Lazzaris' generosity, this trip has cost you almost nothing, so you can afford it. Perhaps you should put all this behind you, scrub your Venice experiences from your memory, and see if Firefly or LittleDutchBoy are in the mood for visitors …

To reconnect with your sculptor and discover if he still wants to get hands-on, go to page 57.

To contact Firefly and see if there's still fire where there's smoke, go to page 245.

You've decided to head to New York to see Firefly

One of the things you like about Firefly is that he's the only one who hasn't seen a photograph of you. The Count and LittleDutchBoy both requested profile pics immediately, and you appreciate that Firefly seems to like you for your personality, and isn't basing his opinion on your selection of carefully chosen shots.

It takes you about twenty tries to get the message just right. In the end you settle on:

<Hey, about what you said . . . I'm thinking, why not? Let's meet! I'll come to NYC>

The second you send it, you're racked with doubt. Did you sound too desperate? Too direct? Too nonchalant? You can't decide. Firefly usually replies immediately, but no message pings back. What if he wasn't serious about meeting you?

You hold your breath.

Ten minutes pass.

Then twenty. You tell yourself that it doesn't matter.

You trawl the internet, keeping an eye on your lovematch.com inbox. An hour passes. You're convinced that you've overstepped the mark and are about to log off, when:

> <Sory. Duty called. Answer is: ARE U
> KIDDING? CAUSE I wanna meet!!!!! When?
> Where?>

Phew. You're surprised at how relieved you feel, but you're not sure if it's because you've been Googling exclusive NYC boutiques and now have your heart set on visiting the city, or because your ego would have been bruised if he'd ignored you for much longer.

> <Hold on a second>

You hop on to your favourite travel site and scope out air tickets. There's a reasonably priced flight that arrives in NYC on Wednesday afternoon. And what's the worst that can happen? If his personality turns out to be as atrocious as his spelling, you can always do some shopping and enjoy a few nights in the city that never sleeps. Who knows? You could meet, there might be fireworks, and sleeping will be the last thing on your mind. You tap in:

<Can get there on Wednesday?>
<Cool. Hey ... can we meet midnight, Empire
State Building? Like in *An Affair to Remember*?
I'm on shift that day. Only get off at 11>

You approve of the venue. It's romantic and even you should be able to find it – the Empire State Building is pretty hard to miss. You'll just have to hope you don't do a Deborah Kerr and get run over by a taxi en route. Quickly, before you can get cold feet, you book your flight, and, with only a moment's hesitation, a charming but expensive hotel in the Lower East Side, right in the heart of vintage-shop heaven and within walking distance of Chinatown.

<Hey, Firefly, we're on!>
<Gr8!!! Shall I send you my number in case u
get lost?>

That would be the smart thing to do, but not as much fun, you think. *An Affair to Remember* wouldn't have had quite the same impact if Cary Grant and Deborah Kerr had had iPhones.

<Let's keep it mysterious>
<OK. How will I no u? Hey! Why don't we both
carry a red rose and a copy of *Pride and
Pregudice*?>

Not for the first time you wonder if he is aware of
spell-check and auto-correct. But you get the reference.

<Like in *You Got Mail*!>
<Egactly!>

Goodness, you think, this guy's really in touch with
his romantic side. You allow yourself a brief moment
of daydreaming about snuggling up on the couch with
him, watching a Nora Ephron marathon, and maybe
helping him polish his helmet ...

You shuffle your way down the aisle of the plane,
cursing yourself for forgetting to check in online. Your
allocated window seat is right at the back of the plane,
next to the toilets. At least there's an empty seat next
to you. You settle in, and dig out your copy of *Pride
and Prejudice*. You haven't read it in years, and you're
immediately engrossed in Lizzie Bennet's life, skipping

ahead so that you can get to her first meeting with the aloof Mr Darcy.

'Hey.'

You look up to see a tall, rangy guy wearing a black leather jacket sliding into the seat next to you. You generally have bad plane karma – you're usually stuck next to the squalling baby or the gargantuan man who smells of cheese – so you can hardly believe your luck. You try not to stare too blatantly at your new seat-mate's bright blue eyes. He's almost too attractive, handsome enough to take the lead role in a romantic movie or top billing in a TV drama.

He holds your gaze for just a second too long to be merely friendly. 'How you doin'?'

'I'm fine, thanks.'

He nods at your book. 'Any good?'

'It's brilliant. One of those novels you can read over and over again.'

'Huh. I'm more of a Lee Child kinda guy myself, but I've always wanted to give the classics a try. But hey, don't let me disturb you.'

'Not at all.' You usually try to avoid small talk on planes, but you reckon you'll make an exception in this case. Pointedly, you close your book.

'So,' he says. 'You going to New York City on vacation, or travelling for business?'

'Pleasure,' you say. Hopefully pleasure of all kinds …

'That's what I like to hear. You know the city?'

'Not really.'

'You're gonna love it. You want me to give you some pointers? I grew up in the Bronx.'

'That would be great, thanks.'

You're barely aware of the plane taking off as he runs through a list of the areas to avoid, hints for taking the subway, and recommendations for non-touristy restaurants and coffee shops.

'What line of business are you in?' you ask.

He hesitates. 'Let's just say I do a lot of travelling.'

'Mysterious. Are you a travel writer?'

'Nothing that glamorous. How about you?' He's dodged the question, but you decide not to press him on it, and briefly tell him about your background and the work you do. He appears to be genuinely interested in what you have to say, and the conversation flows. You're having such a great time, you have to catch yourself and remember exactly why you're going to NYC in the first place. Flirting with tall, dark and handsome fellow passengers wasn't supposed to be on the agenda. *Think of the fireman, think of the fireman.*

But who can blame you for encouraging your travel companion just a little? He's spectacularly good-looking, charming and gregarious, and he smells of leather and spice. And you're not the only one who's noticed. One of the flight crew, a well-groomed diminutive man whose trousers are a size too small, lingers a little too long with the drinks trolley.

Your neighbour orders a Coke Lite, and you opt for a bottle of sparkling water so that you don't look like a lush. The flight attendant tears himself away and moves on to the next row.

You pause, mid-sip, as a voice rises above the background engine noise: 'What is this crap? Give me a glass of champagne now!'

'Sir, that's impossible,' the flight attendant replies. 'Please calm down.'

'I *said*, give me some champagne. Right away.'

'Sir, I've told you, the champagne is for our club and first-class passengers only.'

A baby two rows in front of you starts howling, disturbed by the raised voices. You unclick your belt and peer over the top of the seats. The loud-mouthed man – a shaven-headed guy with a wrestler's build, who's seated at the end of a middle row – leaps to his feet. The flight attendant raises his palms defensively. 'Please sit down, sir.' His chin is wobbling.

'I'd like to see you try and make me.' The big man's voice is slurred – he's obviously had one drink too many already.

The next second, your seat-mate strides down the aisle to the scene of the stand-off.

The troublemaker clenches his fists. 'Who the fuck are you?'

'Marshal Wallace. On-board security. Sit down and calm yourself immediately, or I'll be forced to take action.'

So that explains why he was being cagey about what he did for a living. You've heard that air marshals are supposed to remain anonymous.

The troublemaker jabs a finger in the air marshal's chest. 'Oh yeah? You think you can take me on?'

Lightning-quick, your neighbour grabs the guy's wrist and twists it up behind his back.

The unruly passenger yelps in pain. 'Okay, okay!'

The air marshal releases his grip, and the shaven-headed man slams his mouth shut and sits down as the surrounding passengers break into applause.

'Don't move,' you hear the air marshal saying to the now sheepish troublemaker. He comes back over to you and gives you a rueful grin. 'Wish we could continue this, but I'd better sit closer to that guy in case he flips out again.'

'Will you arrest him?'

'If he continues to misbehave, I'll charge him with interfering with the flight crew.'

Hmm, you could think of worse things than interfering with this particular air marshal. Stop it, you tell yourself. You're en route to meet Firefly, and one action man is enough, isn't it? But you have to admit there was something incredibly masterful about the way he handled the situation, and you're beginning to feel a little ... heated. You need something to distract yourself. You've noticed there's a new Jason Statham movie listed on the in-flight entertainment selection – a guilty pleasure – but if you don't fancy that, you can always go back to your well-thumbed copy of *Pride and Prejudice*. Or maybe you should just try to nap – you don't know how much sleep you'll be getting once you reach New York ...

If you decide to carry on reading Pride and Prejudice, *go to page 255.*

If you decide to watch the Jason Statham film, go to page 263.

If you curl up in your seat for a nap, go to page 269.

You've decided to reread Pride and Prejudice

Your surroundings disappear as you lose yourself once more in Jane Austen's pithy, witty prose. You've reached your favourite part of the novel – where Elizabeth Bennet pays a visit to the crotchety Lady Catherine de Bourgh. You recline your seat and settle back. You can hardly wait to reach the part where Mr Darcy shows up …

You're in the drawing room at Rosings Park, admiring the vista over verdant lawns and the ha-ha to misty blue hills, when the doors fly open with a crash. It's Mr Darcy, unusually dishevelled. A lock of hair is falling over his forehead, and he's coatless, dressed in breeches, impeccably fitted riding-boots and a fine cambric linen shirt, through which you can see the triangle of dark hair on his chest.

He's clearly in the grip of strong emotion, beating his riding-crop against the smooth leather of one booted leg in agitation. 'My feelings will not be repressed,' he bursts out. 'You must allow me to tell you how ardently I love and admire you.'

You've played this scene so often in your head, and

now and again you've wanted to ring the changes. This is your chance.

'Sir,' you say, rising from your seat. 'You are all talk and no trousers.'

His face shows utter mystification.

'What I mean,' you say clearly, 'is that I see no demonstrable signs of your ardour. You profess love, but I have no tangible proof. I demand a sign of your affection.'

Darcy crosses the room in three strides, takes your hand in his, and crushes it to his mouth. His warm lips and breath on the back of your hand send a current racing around your nerve endings, and when he turns your hand and begins kissing the tender skin of your wrist, actual goosebumps pop up.

His mouth travels a little further up ... then a little further ... and when he reaches the tender hollow at the bend in your arm, you whimper aloud. Immediately, his head comes up, alarm in his eyes.

'I beg your pardon – have I offended you?' he asks.

'Only when you stopped,' you say, offering your arm again. This time his mouth inches slowly up the delicate inner stretch between your elbow and your armpit. He pauses momentarily as he encounters the little sleeve of muslin that anchors your empire-line gown to your shoulders, then bypasses it to arrive at your collarbone. Here there's an electric pause, and you can almost hear him wondering whether he dare drop down to your breasts, laced from below into mounds bursting from the neckline of your dress, or up to your lips.

You solve his dilemma by folding your fingers around the back of his neck and tugging slightly, and with a groan, he brings his mouth up to kiss you. For a few seconds, he tries to restrain himself, simply resting his lips chastely against yours, but you melt into him, tipping your hips up against him and softening your mouth invitingly, and he abandons all notions of decorum, opening your lips wide and darting his tongue into your mouth, almost devouring you.

You're almost purring with smugness (you always knew there was a tiger lurking behind that haughty exterior) and pleasure, standing on tiptoes as he explores your mouth thoroughly, but he's slightly too tall for you to hold this pose for long, and you glide backwards until you feel Lady Catherine's pianoforte – her pride and joy – behind you.

Darcy moves with you, but he's puzzled – until you

brace yourself on his shoulders, and hop up on to the edge of the piano. His eyes flare with shock as you open your legs under your skirt, and reach a hand around to his beautifully taut buttocks, toned from all the time he spends in the saddle, and pull him between your invitingly splayed legs.

'Surely you cannot – you do not mean – I cannot possibly ravish you like this!' he splutters.

'Why not?' you say, rolling up your gauzy skirt. Fortunately you remember reading that while ladies of the Regency wore underclothing in the form of chemises and petticoats, they did not wear drawers or bloomers – these were considered terribly shocking, because they outlined the shape of the legs. So under the fine layers of fabric, you're temptingly bare.

Darcy has been seized by a thought. 'Once I have ruined you, you will have no choice but to accept my proposal. In fact, if I confess to your father, he will insist upon our marrying post-haste. Or he will have to challenge me to a duel. You would never place him in such peril, so you shall be obliged to accompany me to the altar.' His eyes glitter. 'So let me have at you, madam.'

You smile, catlike, from under half-closed lids, lean

back, draw your skirt still higher, and open your legs a little wider – just enough to give him a glimpse of the mysterious shadows and folds within.

His throat moves convulsively, and he begins to fumble with the buttons of his breeches, then simply tears them open, releasing a magnificent and very swollen cock. At the sight of it, lust thumps through your lower body, and you open your thighs even wider, bundling your skirt up above your waist.

Darcy's eyes almost leap out of his head, even more so when you reach down to touch your pussy lips, shivering at the slick wetness you find. With your fingers moist from your own juices, you reach for his shaft, and squeeze, then tug his penis gently closer to you. You're both too hungry for foreplay, and you rock your hips up to meet him, and he makes a strangled noise as the head of his cock makes contact with your opening.

'Dear God, you feel like liquid silk,' he chokes, and then he's hammering home, and you're the one groaning, he's so big, too big, and then he's all the way inside you, and your pussy recovers from the shock of his impetuous penetration and stretches, a wonderfully satisfying sensation.

You keep one finger rotating on your clit, as you're hungry to come before he does, and you have a feeling this is going to be a wild and short ride. Yet he keeps thrusting and thrusting, displaying iron control, until your entire universe has contracted to his cock inside your pussy, his slow, deep movements, rings of sensation circling in your lower body, heat coming to the boil.

You're at the stage of tipping over into an orgasm when you become aware of another voice: 'Darcy, you rogue! I intended to pay my addresses to her!' It's Darcy's cousin, Colonel Fitzwilliam! But it's too late for shock or modesty – Darcy's huge cock and the magic it's working on your body is all-encompassing, and you're beginning to spasm, release racking through your body as you shudder your way through a noisy and prolonged orgasm.

Dimly, you're aware out of the corner of one eye that the Colonel has fumbled his breeches open with the clumsiness of a man accustomed to being dressed by a valet, and is yanking at his own, less sizeable, but still impressive erection. As Darcy continues to fuck your convulsing body, Colonel Fitzwilliam subsides into a chair, openly masturbating.

And then it's Darcy's turn: his pupils widen, turning his stormy eyes almost black, and he shoots spurt after spurt of hot come into your twitching pussy, before collapsing on to your prostrate body. But even then, he's a gentleman, taking just enough weight on his arms so that he doesn't crush you.

His gasps have a counterpoint in the Colonel's groans and the thudding of your heart. You're aware of Darcy's semen starting to trickle out of you, feeling like warm oil on your sensitised tissues. Tough about the piano, though.

At that moment, there's another crash and a screech. Lady Catherine de Bourgh is standing surveying the scene, purple-faced and pop-eyed with horror.

'How dare you pollute the shades of Rosings thus!' she shrieks. For a second, you wonder if she's going to drop dead of apoplexy, but instead, she grabs Darcy's abandoned riding-crop. 'You all deserve to be horse-whipped!' she yells, and lays into Darcy's bare and vulnerable backside with all the force she can muster.

Howling with pain, Darcy leaps off you, but ever-chivalrous, he grabs you as you flop on your back on the piano, naked from the waist down, and flips you over. Your legs are too weak to support you, and you hang on to the piano for dear life, your skirt still above your waist.

Another muffled cry indicates that the Colonel has either achieved the heights or fallen foul of Lady Catherine's whip, and now it's your turn. You hear the rustle of her skirts as she marches towards you, a sitting duck as you sprawl over the piano, still panting. You flinch as you anticipate the crop descending on to the tender skin of your buttocks – but there's a pause.

In a hoarse voice, Lady Catherine says, 'I have always found you pert, miss. Your pert breasts ... and now these pert nethers ...' A hand – too small to be Darcy's – comes down to stroke your bare bottom. But why is the piano rocking?

Go to page 269.

You've decided to watch the Jason Statham movie

The film is trashy and fast-paced and you're enjoying every second of it. And there's something about Jason Statham's confidence, his swagger and his swimmer's body that reminds you of the air marshal. A car-chase soundtrack buzzing in your ears, you relax back in your seat and close your eyes.

An ear-piercing scream snaps you out of your reverie. 'Somebody help him!' the flight attendant screeches.

You look up to see the air marshal staggering down the aisle towards you, his unbuttoned shirt revealing a ridged stomach, a sheen of sweat on his forehead. He makes it to your seat, and stares down at you, a panicked look clouding those blue eyes. 'I need you.'

'What is it?'

'I've been poisoned.'

'What?'

'I'm working with a secret government agency. I know too much. They've got to me – must've put something into the in-flight meal.'

Thank goodness you turned down the chicken

lasagne and beef bourguignon with green beans. 'What can I do?'

'I have to flood my system with adrenalin and increase my heartbeat, or I'm going to die.'

'What? Are you sure? That makes absolutely no logical sense.'

'I know it sounds crazy, but please help me – you're the only one I can trust.'

Shell-shocked faces peer over the seats at you. Then it hits you. Haven't you seen a similar scenario in an old Jason Statham movie? You think back – yes, you have, and you realise you know exactly what to do. You stand up, grab the lapels of the air marshal's shirt and press your lips to his. The surrounding passengers gasp. 'Better?' you ask.

'I think so. But I'm going to need more to raise my heartbeat.'

'Don't worry,' you say, feeling your own pulse quicken. Someone has to step up, and it might as well be you. 'Hurry,' you call. 'Help me get him into a bathroom.'

'They're all occupied,' the flight attendant sobs. 'The lasagne . . .'

You round on him. 'Is there anywhere else we can go? Quick, this man's life is at stake.'

'There's a private area at the back of the plane that the crew uses.'

'Take us there now.'

You wrap an arm around the air marshal's waist and help him hobble to the back of the plane and through a small hidden door.

'I'm getting weaker,' he whispers. You pause to kiss him again.

The crew area is tiny, containing nothing but two narrow bunks separated by a curtain. There's something about a near-death experience that's making you feel more alive than ever before – even if it isn't your own near-death experience.

And you're not the only one who's feeling more alive. Despite his weakened condition, you've noticed the telltale bulge in the air marshal's jeans – a bulge that has nothing to do with the holstered weapon at his hip.

There's no time for foreplay, not that either of you need it.

'Lie back,' you instruct. You know you need to keep him as excited as possible to keep him alive. It's a matter of national security. Not to mention that he's damn hot, and you've wanted to do this since the second you laid eyes on him.

'I can't,' he says. 'I need to keep my heart rate accelerated, otherwise my heart will stop beating.'

'Oh, don't worry,' you say, 'I'll keep your heart rate accelerated all right.' With that you drop to your knees at the side of the bed and make quick work of his belt and button, and then his zip and underpants. You draw out his cock, and take it in your mouth.

'Oh my God, that'll do it,' Wallace says, his voice gruff.

You run your tongue up and down his shaft, which is average in length, but very thick, and getting harder by the second.

'Oh my God,' Wallace says again, as you cup his balls and give them a little squeeze. Then you get to work, sliding your mouth up and down over the head of his penis, using your tongue to trace the sensitive tip, as your hand massages his shaft.

Maybe you'll get a medal for saving his life – and for giving the best blowjob ever. Wallace is starting to groan louder and louder, which is a good sign for your best-blowjob-ever medal, but a bad sign if you're meant to be saving his life. If he has an orgasm, surely his heart rate will drop afterwards and he'll die? So you're just going to have to fuck this guy all the way to New York. You've had worse jobs.

You straighten up, and drop kisses all over his face and neck as you fumble with your clothes. The air marshal helps, undoing the buttons of your shirt while you pull off your panties. You unclasp your bra, presenting your breasts to him. 'You're incredible,' he says, reaching for you, 'my heart is racing.'

'We'd better keep it that way,' you say, and then you climb on top of him, facing towards his feet, and lower your pussy on to his face, while you drop your mouth back down on to his erection.

He takes to your pussy like a duck to water. You feel his tongue lashing the length of your slit, probing, and he wraps his arms around your thighs so he can better control your position over his face before pushing his tongue inside you.

His cock is even harder than it was before, and you feel it pulsing with power as you take it in your mouth once again. This time, you wrap both hands around the base of the shaft and suck it in slowly, pumping your mouth to the rhythm of his tongue going in and out of your cunt. Then you feel his fingers applying pressure on your clit, the double sensation making your entire body thrum.

Reluctantly, you tear yourself away from that magic combination of tongue and fingers, and slide down his body, still facing away from him, and guide his cock inside you. Slowly you lower yourself on to him, and start to ride him reverse-cowboy-style, both your hands on his legs, both his hands on your bum and hips. As you ride and ride, you're still aware that you can't risk him coming, so you try to slow down, to vary the speed of your movements, not to get into too much of a rhythm. But then it's too good, and you build up speed until he's pounding hard inside you, and your pussy is starting to contract with an orgasm that's about to rock your body like an earthquake, and you throw your head back as everything really does start to move. The air marshal must be having the orgasm of a lifetime – his thrusts are throwing you around like a rag doll.

Go to page 269.

The plane jolts and you jerk awake. Oh no. Not only is the plane bucking its way through some serious turbulence – which you don't enjoy at the best of times – on its descent, but at some point the air marshal returned to his seat, and you've been leaning against his shoulder. Drooling. You sit up, fish for your bottle of water and take a sip.

'Good nap?' he asks with a smile.

'Um … yes,' you say, blushing scarlet. 'Sorry I fell asleep on you.'

'No problem. It was rather cute – you were talking in your sleep.'

'I was? Did I say anything … embarrassing?'

'Depends what you classify as *embarrassing*.'

You're not sure you want to know. Now would be a good time to change the subject. 'What happened to that guy? The one who was causing a disturbance?'

'He quietened down in the end and apologised. I might let this one go.'

You're silent until the plane touches down twenty minutes later, and the captain runs through his spiel about not leaving your seat until the plane has finished taxi-ing to the gate. The second he stops speaking, everyone gets to their feet and starts rooting through the overhead compartments.

'Hey,' the air marshal says to you, 'how about we swap numbers? I'm thinking we could grab a coffee in that cool place I was telling you about, and I could tell you more about the city.'

You consider it. A coffee would be harmless, wouldn't it? And it would be great to get an insider's view of Manhattan before meeting Firefly. But you have to admit there's also a sneaky part of you that's thinking that if it doesn't work out with the fireman, then …

'Why not?' you say. You give him your phone number, and add his to your contacts under the name 'sxy marshal'.

He stands up and hauls both your bags from the overhead compartment, giving you the perfect opportunity to admire his lean torso once again. 'Hope to see you later,' he says, more than a little meaningfully. 'It was a pleasure to meet you, ma'am.'

'Sorry for the drool,' you blurt out as he joins the crowd exiting the plane, but thankfully he doesn't seem to hear you.

Still feeling slightly groggy from your nap, you head through Immigration and collect your suitcase. You keep an eye out for the air marshal, but it looks like he must have taken a different route through Customs. You join the queue of people waiting for taxis, watching with amusement as the troublemaker is collected by a surprisingly sweet-faced woman, her Chevy sporting a bumper sticker reading: 'Be nice to America or we'll bring democracy to your country.'

As the taxi controller waves you towards the next available cab, your eye is drawn to a swarthy guy in a tailored black overcoat standing near the exit doors. He's not quite as tall as the air marshal, but he certainly has as much presence, and he appears to be checking you out. You stare back at him, but his brooding expression doesn't change – Mr Darcy rather than Jason Statham, you think. After a couple of seconds, he slides on a pair of mirrored shades and turns away. Part of you is relieved. You've already flirted with one random stranger on the flight here; two could be classified as greedy.

Your taxi streams on to the highway and you chit-chat with the driver, a loquacious guy who hails from Mumbai. He agrees to take you the scenic route for no extra charge, and slows so that you can appreciate your first glimpse of the Manhattan skyline. As he drives you along the Williamsburg Bridge, you make out the art-deco curves and the spire of silvery steel that tops the iconic Chrysler Building, and the squarer shoulders and needle-point tip of the Empire State Building, familiar from a thousand movies and TV shows, dominating a sea of equally familiar sky-scrapers. The day is brightening, the sky is a polished blue, and sunlight ripples on the river below. A ferry's horn parps, and to your left, a boat jammed with tourists putters towards Staten Island.

Your phone's message alert beeps. It's a text from the air marshal: 'Great to meet you. Let me know when you want me to buy you that coffee xx.'

That was fast. And he can spell, which is a bonus. Not to mention the two kisses. You decide not to respond immediately – you don't want him to think you're too eager.

The second your taxi leaves the bridge, you're swal-lowed by traffic, the sound of honking horns and raised voices making your pulse beat faster. You're really here! Your driver slices down side streets seem-ingly at random, and you catch sight of Chinatown's multicoloured signage and flag decorations in the distance. Within minutes, he pulls up outside an elegant brownstone.

You pay the driver, thank him for the whirlwind tour, and breathe in your first lungful of New York air. You were expecting the city to reek of traffic fumes or even garbage, but instead you inhale the scent of charred pretzels from a nearby vendor, and as you wheel your bag towards the hotel entrance, you detect the odour of grinding metal wafting up from a subway vent. The sidewalks and streets are as busy as you anticipated; crowds of people weave and hum around you. Everyone seems to have a purpose or a death wish. You pause to watch a couple of businessmen jaywalking across the street, phones glued to their ears, oblivious to the traffic.

Thank goodness you splurged on the hotel, you think, as you admire its recently restored façade, sash windows and metal fire-escape stairs, which adorn the building like false eyelashes. You check in, and are shown to your room, which is far more spacious than you'd hoped, although the window looks out on to a tenement rather than the skyline you'd been imagining.

So what now? Are you going to freshen up and then take a nap? There's plenty of time before your meeting with Firefly. But you don't have that long in the city – do you really want to waste a second? Those exclusive boutiques are calling …

If you decide to take a shower and have a nap, go to page 275.

If you decide to head out straight away, go to page 283.

You strip off your clothes, run the water until it steams, and climb into the spacious shower. The powerful water jets caress your skin, and as you soap your breasts and thighs, an image of the air marshal's lean, muscular body flashes into your mind. No, you think, not a good idea. You turn the water to cold. You have hours to kill before your assignation with Firefly, and you don't want to use up all your energy. You dry off and unpack your case. Hmm, the little black dress you've brought along is creased. It looks like you'll have to explore those boutiques after all. And really, why would you waste your first day in the city that never sleeps by sleeping?

You scoop up your bag and run down to the lobby. The quiet interior immediately makes way for the blare of traffic as you push through the doors. You stand stock still and take it all in for a few seconds. On the other side of the street you catch sight of an overcoated figure standing in the doorway of a laundromat. Hang on ... isn't that the guy you saw outside the airport? The Mr Darcy-ish fellow? It can't be. You take a step forward to get a better look, but then a truck pulls up, obscuring your view. When it draws away, there's no sign of him.

You shrug. Either it's a coincidence or you're going crazy.

You decide to head towards Canal Street and the Bowery, wandering down side streets lined with smoke-sooted buildings. You stop at a little deli-cum-coffee shop that smells tantalisingly of baking bread and roasting coffee beans, and wolf down a bagel, somehow managing not to drown yourself in cream cheese.

Feeling a little more fortified, you decide to ramble wherever your feet take you, but you don't get far – an enticing window display two doors down from the deli catches your eye. The boutique's mannequins are scantily clad in gorgeous and clearly expensive French lingerie. If something was to happen with Firefly, it would do wonders for your confidence if you were kitted out in French lace, and besides, you rationalise, your credit card hasn't had a bashing in ages.

The sales assistant, an elderly woman dressed in an Oleg Cassini suit, greets you warmly. You relax; you were worried that a shop as exclusive as this one would be staffed by intimidating and snobbish sales clerks. 'Are you looking for something special?' she asks.

'Maybe,' you say. 'I have a big night ahead.'

She smiles conspiratorially at you. 'Please, take your time.'

You're immediately drawn to a rack of boned basques that lace up at the back.

'Ah yes,' the saleswoman croons. 'Those are extremely popular, and surprisingly comfortable.' Without looking at the price tag, you choose one in pale pink. It reminds you of something out of the eighteenth century.

The sales assistant waves you towards a curtained-off area in the far corner of the shop, and you slip behind it, unbutton your blouse, unhook your bra, and wriggle into the basque. The saleswoman knows her stuff – it really is surprisingly comfortable. She helps you lace it up at the back, then gestures for you to check out your reflection in the gilt-edged oval mirror. 'It's incredible,' you breathe. It makes your waist look tiny, and you're amazed you can actually breathe in it.

'I have just the thing to go with it,' the saleswoman says. She returns bearing a pair of silk

French knickers, demure yet sexy. They're not really your sort of thing, but you decide to try them anyway, and you step out of your skirt and slip them over your g-string.

You push the changing-room curtain aside to ask the saleswoman's opinion. 'What do you—?'

You bite back a scream as you stare straight into the eyes of the overcoated man who was watching you outside the airport.

'You!' you blurt. 'Are you following me?'

'Yes.' He digs in his inside pocket and flips an official-looking ID card at you. 'Special Agent Bourne from Homeland Security. Ma'am, I'm going to ask you to please come with me.'

'*What?*' You look around for the sales assistant, but she's over in the corner dealing with a pair of Botoxed women who are rifling through the racks of push-up bras. She gives you a little wave.

'I didn't want to cause a disturbance, so I told her I was your husband,' the guy says.

'How dare you!' you manage. His gaze shifts to your breasts, which are spilling over the top of the corset. You cross your arms over your chest, scrabbling to hold on to your dignity. You're still struggling

278

to make sense of this. 'What is all this about?' Did you forget to pay for your bagel? But they'd hardly call in Homeland Security for that.

'Ma'am, please don't make a scene.'

'What do you expect me to do? Agent ...'

'Bourne.'

You snatch his ID card out of his hand. It looks genuine, but what do you know? You take your time scanning it, then look up at him. 'Seriously? Your name is Jason Bourne?'

He sighs. 'It's unfortunate, but yes.'

'So this is your Bourne identity?' You know the last thing you should be doing right now is making lame puns, but you tend to speak without thinking when you're feeling nervous. And being apprehended by a government agent when you're half-naked would unnerve anyone.

He doesn't look amused. 'You can call my field office to ensure I am who I say I am.'

Yeah right, you think. Like you're going to call Homeland Security and ask if Jason Bourne is one of their agents. 'Am I under arrest?'

He sighs. 'No, ma'am. But I'd rather not discuss the situation here.' He glances at the shop assistant and the new arrivals, then his eyes hover over your scantily clad body again. 'Maybe you should get dressed first, and then we'll talk.'

You go scarlet. He's right. You're feeling vulnerable enough as it is. Hands shaking slightly, you close the curtain, and fumble behind you to unlace the basque. Your fingers grasp at the ribbons, but you'd have to be a contortionist to reach them. You poke your head through the curtain, and try to get the saleswoman's attention. She's busy ringing up what has to be several hundred dollars' worth of lingerie for the well-heeled customers.

'You'll have to help me,' you say frostily to the agent. 'I can't undo this thing on my own.'

Pokerfaced, he nods and slips through the changing-room curtain to join you. The already tiny space immediately feels half the size. Wordlessly, you turn your back to him, trying not to think about the absurdity of the situation. He's forced to stand so close, you can feel his breath stirring the tiny hairs on the back of your neck. You're acutely aware of his fingers brushing against your skin as he unravels the ribbons, his touch cool on the sensitive area between your shoulder blades.

'All done,' he says briskly, and you turn to reach for your clothes. But before you can catch it, the basque falls to the floor, and you're left standing in only the silky French knickers, covering your breasts with your hands. Agent Bourne bends to pick up the corset, but you can't take it from him without dropping your hands. You nod to the small chair in the corner of the changing area. 'Just put it there.'

'I'll see you outside,' he says, his voice husky.

You throw on the rest of your clothes, regretfully hand the basque to the bemused saleswoman, and step out on to the street.

Agent Bourne is leaning against a sleek black car with tinted windows, looking every inch an agent out of Central Casting. But if he thinks you're getting in that car, ID card or not, he can think again. 'I'm not getting in there,' you say. 'For all I know this could be an elaborate scam, and you could be a human trafficker.'

'Ma'am ...'

The driver's door opens and an attractive woman with flawless *café-au-lait* skin and cropped hair jumps out. She grins at you and holds out a hand. 'Hello,' she says. 'I'm Agent Petersen. Customs and Border

Protection.' Feeling your mouth dropping open, you take her outstretched hand.

'She says she won't get in the vehicle,' Agent Bourne says to the woman, who grins again, revealing even white teeth. She's far more than just attractive, you think – she's gorgeous.

'I don't blame her,' she says, and waves towards the nearby deli. 'How about we talk in there? And please, call me Isis.'

You find yourself agreeing to her suggestion. At least you'll be in a public place, and besides, you're curious to find out what all this is about.

Go to page 289.

You've decided to head out to go shopping

There's something about the city's pulse that's energising. You stride along, drinking in the atmosphere, slowing every so often to window-shop. You pause to buy a hot pretzel from a vendor, and munch it as you wander at random, licking salt off your fingers. Then you stop dead, your attention caught by a red dress displayed in the window of an intimate vintage clothing store. It's fifties pin-up style, cut to cling in all the right places, and it looks to be just your size.

Your breath gives a little hitch. You'd look amazing in that. And you have just the right heels to go with it. You hurry inside, where you're greeted by a large and cheerful middle-aged woman with black bobbed hair and bright-pink lipstick.

'The red dress in the window,' you say. 'It's fabulous.'

'Isn't it?' she gushes. 'It's a Ceil Chapman.' She appraises you. 'Would you like to try it on?'

'Please.' You wait while the assistant wrestles it off the mannequin, running your fingers through the racks of timeless clothes. The shop smells of perfume and old paper.

The bell trings and you turn to see a breathtakingly beautiful woman with short black hair entering the store. She's dressed in jeans and high boots, and the red silk scarf tied around her neck adds to her aura of effortless chic – she's the kind of woman who usually makes you feel dowdy. She gives you a friendly smile, and starts clacking through the racks.

The sales assistant hands you the dress and directs you to the changing-room, explaining that you'll have to use the mirror in the main area of the shop.

You wriggle into the dress, but you can't reach high enough to inch the zip up all the way. You step out into the shop, and the gorgeous woman glides up to you.

'Here, let me,' she says. While the saleswoman hovers, she zips you in and pulls down the hem of the dress. Catching your eye in the mirror, she smooths the fabric over your hips. You flush – if anyone but this woman had done this to you, you'd have been aghast at their presumption.

'Perfect,' the shop assistant enthuses.

'No,' your fellow customer says. 'It's not quite right.' Her accent is pure New York.

You cock your head and turn to check out the back

of the dress. You have to agree with her. It's slightly too tight under the arms. You sigh in disappointment. It was worth a try.

'Thanks,' you say regretfully, heading back into the changing-room.

You're still in your underwear when the chic woman pokes her head through the curtain. 'I hope you don't mind,' she says, 'but I spotted something that I thought would look magnificent on you.'

She steps inside, filling the space with a spicy, exotic perfume, and holds up a sky-blue twenties-style dress, a row of intricate covered buttons down the back – something you would never pick out for yourself.

'I'm not sure it's my colour ...'

She smiles. 'Why not try it? Trust me. Here, let me help you. Hold up your arms.'

You're not sure what to make of this, but you do as she says and let her slide the dress over your head, the silky fabric cool against your skin, her fingers lightly brushing your waist and hips as she inches the fabric down, making you shiver.

'Turn around so that I can do you up.'

As she fastens the buttons, one by one, every so often the tips of her fingers whisper against your back.

Her touch is light and, dare you say it, sensual. You're pretty sure she's coming on to you, but for some reason you don't find this intrusive.

'There.' She stands back to assess you, licking her lips. 'Go out and take a look.'

You step out of the changing-room and check out your reflection. You hardly recognise yourself. The colour makes your eyes sparkle and the bias cut of the dress flatters your curves.

'Your friend has good taste,' the sales assistant says.

'Oh, she's not my friend. We've only just met.'

Expecting the gorgeous woman to be behind you, you turn to thank her, but she's nowhere to be seen. You peer into the changing-room and gasp. She's ... she's rooting through your bag!

'Hey!' you shout.

She holds her hands up. 'Ma'am, it's not what you think.'

'Call the cops,' you yell at the sales assistant. 'This woman is trying to rob me.'

The woman in question digs in her pocket and retrieves an ID card. 'There's no need for that. I *am* the cops.'

'*What?*'

286

'Special Agent Isis Petersen from Customs and Border Protection. I'm going to have to ask you to come with me.'

'Excuse me? You're who from what?'

She repeats herself patiently. 'Agent Isis Petersen from Customs and Border Protection. Ma'am, I have reason to believe that you may be involved in some malfeasance.'

Customs and Border Protection? You cast your mind around for some mysterious infraction that might have caught their attention – surely they're not after you for the jar of emergency Nutella you brought over in your suitcase? And you didn't go *that* wild in duty-free. Could this be some kind of scam?

You put on your best haughty voice. 'What is this about?'

'I'd rather not talk about it here, ma'am.'

'Am I under arrest?'

'No, ma'am. To be honest, I'm here to ask for your help.'

'My help?'

She nods. 'It's important. I'll wait for you outside.'

The saleswoman, who is looking as disconcerted as

you're feeling, helps you unbutton the dress. You throw on your clothes, and hurry out of the store.

Agent Petersen is waiting for you directly outside, leaning against a sleek car with blacked-out windows.

'Ma'am,' a low male voice says behind you. You turn to see the guy from outside the airport. The one who reminded you of Mr Darcy. What on earth is going on? 'We'd appreciate it if you'd come with us.' He hands you an identity card.

'This is Agent Bourne from Homeland Security,' Isis says. 'We're working a case together.'

Now completely bewildered, you check out his identification, noting that his first name is Jason. Jason Bourne? Scam artists wouldn't be that stupid or obvious, would they? Still, there's no way you're getting into a car with these two.

You notice a small deli on the opposite side of the street, close to what looks like a fabulous lingerie store. 'If you want to talk to me, then how about there?'

The inscrutable guy sighs, but Isis grins at you. 'Sounds like a plan.'

Go to page 289.

You go to the deli

You're twitchy with anxiety, so you order coffee and a slice of chocolate fudge cake. Chocolate always calms you when you're nervous. Isis mirrors your order, but Agent Bourne orders a skinny latte and a bran muffin.

'So,' you say, once the waitress leaves. 'What is this all about?'

'Ma'am, would you mind if I looked in your bag?' Isis asks.

'My bag?'

'Please.'

Curious, you hand her your tote, and Isis pulls on a pair of surgical gloves and starts hauling out the contents. Not for the first time, you wish you'd bothered to clear it out. Your copy of *Pride and Prejudice* plops out on the table, along with an old tissue, a battered box of tampons, a theatre ticket from three years ago, a hairbrush that your friend's dog chewed, and several condoms. Agent Bourne eyes them, then gives you an assessing look. You stare back at him defiantly.

'Don't worry, my bag is much worse,' Isis says cheerfully. 'It's a black hole of junk.'

She reaches into one of the interior pouches – the bag has several, but you don't usually use them – and pulls out something you haven't seen before, a small cloth bag. She carefully shakes the contents into a saucer, and a shower of small glassy pebbles spills out. They don't look like anything special – rather grubby fragments of broken glass – and you reach out to touch them.

Agent Bourne catches your hand. 'Don't.'

'What are they?'

'Blood diamonds,' Isis says.

'*Blood diamonds?* Are you serious?'

She certainly looks deadly serious. 'This little haul will fetch hundreds of thousands of dollars on the black market. I'd say we're looking at about fifty carats' worth – probably from Zimbabwe.'

You're dimly aware that blood – or conflict – diamonds are mined in war zones, often by children in horrific conditions, and used to bankroll civil wars and terrorism. Didn't a supermodel's testimony that a warlord had given her a few 'dirty-looking stones' help convict him of war crimes?

'But what the hell are they doing in my bag?'

'You tell us,' Agent Bourne snaps.

'I've got no idea.'

'Why don't you start by telling us why you're in New York in the first place?'

'That's none of your business.'

'Ma'am, you could be in serious trouble here. It would be best if you cooperated with us.'

'I thought you said I wasn't under arrest?'

He sighs and runs his hands through his short dark hair.

'Okay, okay,' you say. 'Um ... I'm here because I have to meet someone at midnight. At the top of the Empire State Building.'

Isis looks bemused, but Agent Bourne says: 'Like in *An Affair to Remember*?' You're surprised he got the reference. Maybe all New York authority figures are in touch with their romantic sides. He takes out a notebook. 'And who is this person? Can you give me his or her name and contact details?'

'I ... I don't have them.' Your cheeks are growing hot. 'It's kind of a blind date. We met online and ...'

'You flew to New York to meet a complete stranger?' Agent Bourne shakes his head, but Isis smiles at you.

'He isn't a complete stranger,' you say defensively.

'I met my ex online,' Isis says. 'It's no big deal, as long as you're careful and stay aware of the pitfalls.' You're beginning to like this woman.

Then something strikes you. 'Shouldn't we be doing this in a police station?'

'We can't,' Isis says. 'We're not entirely sure who else might be involved, or if he has an informant in one of the law-enforcement agencies.'

'He?'

'The man you sat next to on the plane.'

'The hot guy?' You really need to learn to think before you speak. 'He put this in my bag? But ... he's an air marshal.'

'Yeah,' Isis says. 'And he's been using his position to smuggle conflict diamonds into and across the States for years. We've managed to detain the ringleaders in his cartel, but without him, our whole case could fall apart. We think he suspected we were on to him, which is why he placed the contraband in your bag to avoid being caught.'

'At some point he'll want to retrieve the goods,' Agent Bourne chimes in. 'We need your help.'

Isis places a hand over yours. 'You'll be perfectly safe, I promise. Will you help us?'

If you decide it's too dangerous and you don't want to
   be involved, go to page 294.
If you say yes, you'll help them, go to page 295.

You've decided it's too dangerous and you don't want to be involved

Come on. That's pathetic. What sort of a person are you? The least you can do is go straight to http://www.warchild.org/.

Go to page 295.

You've decided you'll help the agents catch the air marshal

'I'll do it,' you say. Isis sighs with relief, and Agent Bourne's stony expression softens. 'What's the plan?'

'Did you tell him where you were staying?' Agent Bourne asks.

'No. But we swapped numbers, and he invited me for coffee.' The agents exchange glances. You dig out your phone and show them the text message, remembering too late that you listed him under the name 'sxy marshal'. You're mortified that you ever thought someone as twisted as Marshal Wallace was hot.

'Can you text him back? Tell him you want to meet?' Isis asks.

Fingers shaking from the effects of adrenalin mixed with sugar and caffeine, you type in the message: 'Hey. Coffee sounds like a great idea.'

The three of you wait for a response in silence. You glance up from your phone to see Agent Bourne assessing you.

'Have I just grown two heads?'

'You've got frosting at the corner of your mouth.' He leans forward and gently wipes it away with his thumb.

Isis looks at him and rolls her eyes. 'Very smooth.'

You jump as your phone buzzes. A message from the air marshal. You read it out to the others: 'Thought you'd forgotten me. Rockefeller Plaza Starbucks, when would suit? xx'.

Starbucks? So much for the intimate coffee shop he'd mentioned. But that's the least of your concerns.

'Tell him you'll be there in thirty minutes,' Isis says.

Hands still trembling, you do as she asks. The reply comes almost immediately: 'It's a date x'.

'We're on,' you say. 'What's next?'

'We wire you up, then get going.'

They usher you to the car, and you numbly climb inside. Agent Bourne extracts a tiny microphone from a steel briefcase, and you unbutton your jacket so that he can pin it on to your blouse. You're certain he can feel the thump of your heart.

'You're doing a good thing here, ma'am,' he says quietly, looking into your eyes. 'Thank you.'

As you walk into the coffee outlet, your heart feels as if it's jumped from your chest into your throat. Agent Bourne and Isis are already sitting at a table in the back, Isis pretending to talk on her phone, Agent

Bourne seemingly lost in his Kindle. You fleetingly wonder what he's reading, but you doubt it's *Pride and Prejudice*. You walk up to the counter and order a long black Americano, wishing there was an option to add a shot of vodka.

'Thanks for meeting me,' a voice says in your ear, making you jump.

You turn to see the air marshal standing way too close to you. His startlingly blue eyes now seem like chips of ice, those chiselled features cruel rather than handsome.

'No problem,' you manage.

'Shall we?'

You follow him to the far side of the room and sit down at a table next to a couple of bickering British tourists. The woman can barely tear her eyes away from the air marshal as he takes his jacket off, revealing a tight black t-shirt. You don't miss that there's a bulge on his right side. And you don't think it's because he's pleased to see you – that's his gun.

'Aren't you warm?' he asks.

'A little.' You don't dare take off your jacket in case he notices the tiny microphone stuck to your blouse. He makes small talk, asking what you've been doing so far. You mumble something about shopping.

'How's your hotel?' he asks.

'Lovely.'

'What district are you staying in?'

'Upper East Side,' you lie. You don't want this guy to know where you're staying. You take a sip of coffee, scalding your tongue – it's way too hot. You glance over at Isis, and she gives you a minuscule nod. This is it. Time to channel your inner Jason Statham or Gina Carano. They make this stuff look easy.

'I'm just going to the bathroom,' you say, fighting to keep your voice steady. 'You don't mind watching my stuff, do you?' You place your tote on the table between you, trying to look casual about it.

He shrugs. 'Sure. No problem.' He barely glances at it. Could the agents be wrong about him? But how else could those diamonds have got into your bag?

You head towards the bathroom on wobbly legs. Agent Bourne and Isis instructed you to leave the scene as fast as possible, but something makes you pause and turn around.

His back to you, the air marshal seizes your bag and digs through it, fishing out the pouch and slipping it into his pocket.

'Hold it right there!' Isis shouts at him.

Time seems to slow. As Isis and Agent Bourne run towards his table, the air marshal spins, pulls out his gun, and points it straight at the female British tourist. Her partner screams and drops under the table; she blanches and wrings her hands, wailing, 'I told you we should've gone to Benidorm!'

'Put the gun down,' Isis says in a steady voice.

'Not gonna happen,' the air marshal says.

It's a stand-off. You're not sure what makes you do it, but before you can think about what could go wrong, you creep forward, grab your coffee and fling it at the back of his head. Startled, the air marshal jumps, drops the gun and clutches the back of his neck, which is turning bright red. That coffee was seriously hot – he must be in agony.

Within seconds, Isis has him on the ground, her knee on his back, her handcuffs already out.

The rest of the customers flee the scene, but you're rooted to the spot. You feel a hand on your shoulder, and look up into Agent Bourne's dark eyes.

'You okay?' he asks, in a low voice.

Are you? You're not sure.

'That was quick thinking. You did good.'

He walks you out of the outlet, the street alive with

the screeches of approaching police sirens. The light is too bright; the raised voices around you hurt your ears. 'You're going to have to come with us to the field office to complete a statement,' Agent Bourne says gently. 'You up for that?'

Shivering as the last traces of adrenalin leave your system, you nod.

The paperwork takes hours, and you're limp with exhaustion by the time Isis and Agent Bourne tell you that the air marshal has made a full confession, and you're free to go. You check the time. Seven p.m. Still a few hours to go before your assignation with Firefly. You're not sure you're really in the mood any more, but it would be cruel to leave him hanging. You gather your things together. Your tote has been taken in as evidence, but Isis has found you an NYPD souvenir bag for all your bits and pieces.

'One of us will give you a lift to your hotel,' Isis says. 'Any preferences?'

If you decide to go with Agent Bourne, go to page 301.

If you decide you'd rather grab a ride with Isis, go to page 317.

You've decided to get a lift with Agent Bourne

For the first few minutes of the drive, neither of you speak. Then, as you clear the Broadway traffic, Agent Bourne asks, 'Hungry?'

You turn to look at him. 'What?'

'Are you hungry?'

Your stomach grumbles, and you realise you're starving. Adrenalin clearly burns a ton of calories.

'I know a great place where we could eat.' He looks over at you and smiles for the first time. It transforms his face, erasing every scrap of his former aloofness. You consider his offer. After all the drama, you're not sure you want to be alone, and maybe he really is a Mr Darcy, all prickly on the outside and soft inside.

'Why not?' you say.

'Great.' He smiles again. 'Listen, I know I must have come across as harsh back there. Professional persona.'

'It's fine,' you say. 'I get it.' You're still a little fragile after your adventure, so you're barely aware of your surroundings until you're heading towards the Williamsburg Bridge, leaving the lights of Manhattan behind.

'Ever been to Brooklyn?' he asks. You shake your head. He tells you about growing up in Brooklyn Heights before it became gentrified and the spiralling house prices eventually displaced most of the locals. 'I moved to Williamsburg a few years back,' he says. 'The neighbourhood is growing on me.'

He drives along a street teeming with little artisanal bakeries, vintage stores and groups of hipsters sipping lattes and smoking. It's an arty neighbourhood, not the kind of place you'd expect someone as seemingly conventional as Agent Bourne to reside. He turns down a side street lined with trees, their leaves starting to turn orange and yellow with the onset of fall, and pulls up outside an apartment block with a bright-red door.

'This is the place?' you say. 'It doesn't look like a restaurant to me.'

He smiles again. 'I've got an errand to run first, if that's okay with you.' He unlocks the door and waves you into a hallway that smells of lavender and frying onions. Your stomach growls again. You follow him up a flight of stairs to another red door, and the second he unlocks it, a bundle of fluff bounds out at you.

You look down at a small white poodle, who's yipping and dancing around Agent Bourne's legs.

'This is Manchee.'

Manchee calms down, sits at your feet and holds up a paw. You drop to your knees and shake it gently.

Agent Bourne smiles approvingly. 'He likes you. He doesn't do that for everyone.'

'He's so cute.' You pet the dog again, then get to your feet. 'I wouldn't have thought you were the poodle type.'

'Yeah, I get that a lot. Manchee used to belong to an elderly neighbour. When she died, I kinda inherited him.'

Now you're on to this guy: his aloofness really is nothing but a façade.

You follow him into his apartment. It's both warm and stark, mirroring what you know of his personality: stripped-brick walls, wooden floors and bookcases heaving with everything from literary fiction to pulpy crime thrillers.

'I have to take Manchee for his walk,' he asks. 'Would you like to join us?'

You nod. Fresh air is exactly what you need. The poodle dancing at your heels, you stroll through the neighbourhood in a strangely companionable silence, heading towards a cluster of abandoned brick factories next to the river. A group of kids swaggering along the opposite side of the street shout greetings at Agent Bourne, and he shares a brief conversation with them in Spanish. You round a corner, and catch sight of the lights of Manhattan gleaming in the distance. Everything feels slightly unreal.

You pause to breathe in chilly air tinged with salt. 'What a day,' you say. And then, with no warning, you start shaking, pressure filling your chest. Unable to stop yourself, you start sobbing.

'Hey,' Agent Bourne says softly, drawing you to him. Fighting to control yourself, you rest your head against his chest, and he wraps his overcoat around you both, the heat of his body warming you. 'It's the shock,' he whispers. 'A delayed reaction. It's perfectly normal.'

It's several minutes before you stop shaking, but you're feeling far more grounded now. You step back, and Manchee jumps up at you, whining. You wipe your eyes and tousle the top of the dog's head.

'I'm sorry,' you say to Agent Bourne. 'I've made your shirt all wet.'

'No problem. I think it's about time we fed you. Shall we head home?'

As you retrace your steps, you question him about his life and career. You learn he joined Homeland Security ten years ago after a spell in the military, and is amicably divorced and childless. You're surprised at how forthcoming he is about his private life, and the walk back to his street is over far too soon.

Back in the apartment, he asks: 'You okay with home cooking?'

'Sounds good.'

He puts on some music – something low and bluesy – and you follow him into the kitchen, which appears to be the largest room in the apartment and is kitted out to a professional standard. The open shelves and racks are crammed with herbs and spices, jars of pulses, and bottles of olive oil.

He feeds Manchee, then pours you a glass of red wine. You take a sip and look around for somewhere to sit.

'Here,' he says. And before you can stop him, he puts his hands around your waist and lifts you up so that you can sit on the spacious counter. 'Keep me company,'

With Manchee lying at his feet, he strips off his jacket, rolls up his sleeves to reveal muscular forearms, and pulls a couple of red onions out of a vegetable rack.

'How do you feel about Cuban food?' he says. 'It's the real thing. My grandmother taught me.'

'I don't know much about it, but the bit about your grandmother sounds like a recommendation.'

You watch as he chops and fries onions, then renders a fragrant bunch of coriander into a finely minced green pile, along with green chillies and garlic, before squeezing fresh lime over it.

'I've got a fresh tuna steak here,' he says. 'I reckon we can share it, with *frijoles negros* – that's black beans – and salsa on the side.'

He dives into his refrigerator, bringing out jars of obviously home-made sauces. Your mouth waters as he smothers the fish in the fresh green herb mix and adds it to the onions, where it pops and sizzles, releasing heavenly aromas.

'Here, try this.' He offers you a spoonful of peppery sauce, then dabs the corner of your mouth with gentle fingers. And then, without warning, he's kissing you, and it feels comforting and natural and incredibly hot, all at the same time. You let go a deep sigh, wrap your arms around his neck and lean into him.

If you don't want to stop, go to page 308.
If you think it might be wiser to stop, go to page 312.

'This is incredibly unprofessional of me. You're a witness,' he murmurs, feathering kisses against your neck. You tilt your head to give him more access. After the shocks of the day, you don't want to think any more – you just want to give yourself over to pure feeling. And the sensation of his mouth nibbling down to your shoulder, then up to your jawline, is all you care about in the here and now.

'But I'm not a professional,' you whisper. 'Surely there's some latitude here?' And you lick gently at the rim of his ear. He shudders, and you wrap your legs around his waist, making it impossible for him to escape.

Then you're kissing again, deeply, clutching each other's backs, then pulling at each other's clothes. 'Wait,' he says, and you whimper, 'Don't want to.' He laughs deep in his throat and reaches out an arm to switch off the gas rings on the stove and shift your wine-glass out of harm's way.

You're fighting your way out of your jacket and unbuttoning your blouse, and his hands reach eagerly for your breasts, still in your bra. You tilt your hips up, jamming them still more firmly against his groin, where there's apparently a boulder in those smartly cut trousers. Abandoning your buttons, you tug at his belt and the opening of his pants, growling with frustration as your fingers fumble. But then you find what you're seeking, the lump of his erect cock springing against you through his underpants, and you dive in to release it.

He groans and returns the favour, scrabbling under your skirt, hooking your knickers and ripping them off so hard the elastic snaps.

Oh God, the condom moment – but he's ahead of you. Fortunately, he remembers where they are, and dives into your replacement bag.

'Look,' he grins as he fishes one out, 'I've found the contraband!'

'Now *that's* a girl's best friend. Much better than diamonds,' you say breathlessly, reaching out to help him put it on.

Then you lean back slightly, one arm still hooked around his shoulders, the other bracing yourself on the counter for his entry. He thrusts hard against you and you gasp as he slides in, almost roughly, pushing deep into you. You hitch your legs higher, wrapping them around his firm backside, and the angle is easier, and you find a rhythm together, beginning to fuck each other hard and strong. The penetration is dirty and lusty, but the kissing that accompanies it is passionately romantic, his lips and tongue soft and tender in contrast to the pure male hardness thrusting up into your pussy.

All too soon, his body jerks repeatedly as he comes with a groan. Still holding you and still inside you, he apologises in between catching his breath. 'That was a bit of a sprint. But how about I take you into the bedroom and show you the slow route?'

Later, when you're lying in his bed, his arms around you, guilt begins to creep up on you. 'I'm supposed to be meeting someone,' you say.

The last thing you want to do is leave, but you can't bear the thought of Firefly waiting alone for you at the top of the Empire State Building.

'How about we find a way to let him know you won't be coming?' Agent Bourne says.

'How? I don't have his number.'

He smiles, reaches for his phone and asks the operator to put him through to the security desk at the

Empire State Building. 'What do you want to say? I can get security to page him.'

You're still feeling faintly guilty about leaving Firefly in the lurch, but you tell yourself you can send him a message tomorrow, apologising for standing him up. 'Tell him that I've been unavoidably detained.'

You snuggle back into Jason Bourne's arms, wondering where, if anywhere, all this will go.

As if he can read your mind, he pulls you on top of him. 'It's not over till it's over,' he says. 'And besides, you'll have to come to New York again for the trial, won't you?'

THE END

You decide it's wiser to stop

You break away from the embrace. You're both breathing heavily and your whole body is trembling. 'I can't,' you say. 'We've only just met. And ...'

'I know. You've got to meet that guy.'

'It would be cruel to leave him hanging like that.'

He detaches himself gently. 'Not to mention that sleeping with a witness isn't exactly good policy. I'm sorry. I shouldn't have come on to you.'

'It's okay.' You slide down from the counter. 'But I'd better go.'

'You can't leave on an empty stomach.'

You suspect that if you stay to eat, you won't be able to resist kissing him again. 'I really have to go,' you say regretfully.

He nods. 'At least let me drive you.'

You consider it, but you're not sure it's good etiquette to allow one potential love interest to deliver you to another potential love interest. 'It's fine. I can use the subway.'

As you button up your jacket, Agent Bourne gives you directions to the nearest subway station. Then, not entirely sure you're making the right decision, you stroke Manchee goodbye, and head out into the night.

'Pelham Bay Park. End of the line,' an automated voice barks.

You look up. Oh no. This isn't your stop. You were supposed to get off at Grand Central Station!

After you left Williamsburg (stopping for a hotdog with all the trimmings en route), you'd taken a quick shower back at your hotel, stepped into your little black dress, and decided to take the subway rather than a taxi to the Empire State Building, rationalising that you had loads of time. But you've been day-dreaming instead of watching the stops, and you've ended up at the end of the line – and God knows where. You jump off the train and ask a group of local kids wearing headphones for directions to your desti-nation. They oblige, and it seems simple enough. You hurry to the other side of the station to catch a train back towards midtown.

You sit on an empty bench, and after ten minutes and no train, there's an announcement that the 6 has been delayed due to 'passenger injury' at Castle Hill. After half an hour, you're twitching with anxiety.

Another five minutes pass, and you decide to leave the station and take a taxi. But the second you reach the top of the stairs, the train draws in – there's no way you'll be able to belt back to catch it in time.

You hurry out of the station, and gaze around at the unfamiliar environment. The area is nowhere near as populated as the Manhattan you're used to, and it's a good twenty minutes before an empty taxi appears, but you fulfil a small ambition by telling the driver to step on it. He obliges, but it still seems to take hours to reach Central Park. The cabby turns on to Broadway, then cuts down a less populated street. You groan: workmen wearing Day-Glo vests are busy cordoning off the area. You're gridlocked.

'How far is it?' you ask the driver.

He gives you directions. You can easily walk it from here, but there's no doubt about it, you're going to be late. Slipping off your heels, you leap out of the cab and run down the sidewalk. Steam hisses up from the underground vents, smelling curiously of laundry detergent, and you bob and weave through a group of guys wearing low-slung jeans, and a gaggle of Korean tourists. You almost barrel into a bevy of drunk businessmen tumbling out of a sushi restaurant. You push your way through them, and taking your life into your hands, you run across Fifth Avenue, dodging taxis and jaywalkers, wincing at the barrage of swearing targeted at you.

Out of breath and sweaty, you fly into the Empire State Building, hurriedly pay the entrance fee, and race into the elevator. 'C'mon, c'mon, c'mon,' you mutter as it inches its way to the top.

'Don't panic, honey,' says the operator, an elderly man with kind eyes. 'If he's worth it, he'll still be there.'

You smile at him gratefully. You step out of the lift, and head towards the main observation deck. It's far larger than you'd imagined, and you realise it would be possible for you to miss Firefly altogether if he was also rambling around, searching for you. Still, at this time of night, there are only a few tourists. Your heart skips a beat as you see a good-looking guy in a bomber jacket leaning against a pillar and glancing at his watch, but then a blonde woman approaches him and they embrace. With the exception of an attractive nail-chewing woman who looks as lost as you feel, the only people you encounter are paired up, and, feeling self-conscious and lonely, you trail along, barely aware of the incredible view. You're feeling almost tearful as you round the last corner. Then, something catches your eye on the floor next to one of the viewfinders – a copy of *Pride and Prejudice* and a crushed rose.

You bend to pick them up. Too late. You're too late.

'Is that you?'

You turn to see a large, bear-like man with a pleasant, craggy face walking towards you.

'Firefly?' you ask hopefully.

'Yeah. That's me.' He's nowhere near as conventionally attractive as the devious air marshal or Agent Jason Bourne, but his dark eyes are warm and expressive, and you feel instantly comfortable with him.

'I'm so sorry I'm late,' you say.

He smiles, crinkles appearing at the corner of his eyes. 'You're here now. And I would have waited for you until morning, if that's what it took.'

Goodness. You doff your hat silently to lovematch.com – it seems you've snagged a genuinely sweet guy. You're relieved you hadn't left him hanging after all.

Go to page 324.

Isis whips through the traffic, braking sharply and taking corners with the skill of a rally driver. 'Tell you what,' she says, pausing to curse at a taxi driver who cuts her off, 'after you've freshened up at your hotel, why don't we grab a bite to eat?'

Why not? you think. You like Isis's company, and it'll save you navigating the subway. It's a shame you didn't manage to buy a dress, but the little black number you packed just in case will have to do.

Isis parks in a red zone a block from your hotel, and places an 'on duty' card on the dashboard. 'Perk of the profession,' she announces.

You can hardly expect her to wait in the car while you get changed, so you invite her up to your room. The receptionist eyes Isis approvingly as you collect your key, obviously thinking you have good taste in companions. As you head up to your floor in the elevator, you're more than aware of the spicy scent of her skin. You hang back to allow her to enter your room first, wondering if you're imagining the charge crackling between you.

'Not bad,' she says, bouncing on the bed. 'Mind if I make myself at home?'

You tell her to go ahead. She removes her jacket, chucks it on to an armchair, grabs the TV remote and lies back on the bed.

'I think I'm going to have a bath, if that's okay,' you say.

'Good idea. And take your time. You've got a few hours to spare.'

You run the bath as hot as you dare, pour in every drop of the complimentary bubble bath, and sink back into the water, feeling the day's tension easing out of your muscles.

'You okay in there?' Isis calls through the door.

You must have dropped off. The bubbles have dissolved, but the water is still warm.

'I'll just be a minute!' You climb out, run a comb through your hair, wrap yourself in a towel and join Isis, perching on the corner of the bed.

'Feeling better?' she asks.

You open your mouth to answer her, and then, out of nowhere, your breath hitches and you start sobbing.

'Hey,' Isis says, scooting across the bed to wrap an arm around you. 'It's fine.'

'I don't even know why I'm crying.'

'It's the shock.' She strokes your neck and you're acutely aware of how warm her hands are.

You draw back and look into her eyes, and then she traces your lips with a finger.

Wait – what are you doing? You have to meet Firefly in a couple of hours.

'I can't,' you say. 'I want to … but I made a promise to someone else.'

Isis sighs, gently disentangles herself and swings her legs off the bed. 'You're right. It would be incredibly unprofessional of me, anyway. You are our star witness, after all.'

'What now?' you ask, wrapping your towel tighter around your still-tingling body.

Isis grins at you. 'How does crispy duck in Chinatown sound?'

'You still want to have dinner with me?'

'Sure. I've been turned down before. I can handle it.'

You very much doubt that a woman as beautiful as Isis has had much experience of rejection, and you're relieved – and, you have to admit, a little bit regretful – that she's taken it so well. You still have a few hours to kill, and your stomach rumbles at the thought of food.

'And I know a great place where we can get an after-dinner drink that's close to your final destination.'

You smile back at her. 'Sounds good.'

The meal was one of the finest you've ever had. The restaurant was set at the far end of Chinatown, behind a discreet black door, and you both gorged yourselves on crispy Peking duck, plum sauce and delicate pancakes. And the bar Isis has chosen – a block from the Empire State Building – is just your sort of place, with comfortable booths and lots of wood panelling. You settle into a booth, and Isis orders a couple of beers.

You take a minute to check out the other patrons, your eye drawn to a large dark-haired guy with broad shoulders sitting by himself at the bar. He's nursing a whiskey and staring straight ahead. Then you notice what's in front of him: a copy of *Pride and Prejudice* and a red rose. As if he can sense your eyes on him, he turns and stares at you. Wordlessly, you dig in your bag and hold up your own copy.

He gapes, recovers, and then his face breaks into a broad grin. He stands up and approaches your table.

Isis gives you a look. 'You know this guy?'

'Firefly?' you say to him. He nods. He isn't as stereotypically handsome as Jason Bourne or the evil air marshal, but there's something confident about the way he holds his body. A strong, craggy face, but kind eyes. You'd kind of hoped that he'd be wearing his fireman's outfit, but beggars can't be choosers.

He glances questioningly at Isis, obviously curious as to why you're accompanied by possibly the hottest woman in New York. You introduce him to her, and she gathers her stuff together. 'I'd better go. Let you two continue your evening alone.'

If you say farewell to Isis, go to page 322.
If you ask her to stay for one more drink, go to page 330.

You say farewell to Isis

You walk Isis to the door. 'Thanks for everything,' you say to her.

'I should be the one thanking you. If it wasn't for your quick thinking, that situation in the coffee shop would have gotten messy.' She hands you her card, lightly stroking your palm as she does so. 'And if it doesn't work out with your fireman, you know who to call ...'

'Thanks. It's been ...' You search for the right word. 'Different.'

She smiles, leans forward and gently kisses your cheek. 'Good luck. I'll be in touch.'

As you watch her walk away on a tide of lascivious glances from the other bar patrons, you can't help wondering what might have been.

You slide back into the booth and share a smile with Firefly. You realise you're immediately comfortable with this man, as if you've known each other for ages.

'I thought you didn't know anyone in New York,' Firefly says.

You take a deep breath. 'It's a long story,' you say,

launching into the adventures of the day. He's a great listener and as someone clearly used to working with law enforcement, he asks all the right questions. Once you wind up your tale, he reaches across the table and takes your hand. 'You must be exhausted.'

You realise the last thing you feel like doing right now is sleeping. 'Actually, I'm wide awake.'

'Well then,' he says, 'we're right here. Why don't we head up to where we were supposed to meet?'

'It would be a shame not to.'

As you head across the street, he takes your hand. His palm is warm and swallows yours, and you realise you feel completely safe with him.

Go to page 324.

You peer through the bars at the top of the building and gaze over the city. The Chrysler Building's lights cast a halo of colour around its top.

'What a view,' you breathe.

'I'll say,' Firefly says. 'I never get tired of it.' He hitches an arm round your shoulders. 'Hey, I wanted to say thanks for not judging me on my godawful spelling. I'm a little dyslexic.' He holds up his hands. They really are enormous. 'It doesn't help that these fingers aren't great with keyboards.'

You both watch as an out-of-breath man runs out of the elevator, glances around and races over to a nervous-looking woman you spotted as you arrived. They exchange a few halting words, then embrace.

'Looks like we weren't the only ones who had this idea,' you say.

Firefly smiles. 'Wait here.'

'Where are you going?'

'Give me a minute.'

He disappears into the observation-deck lobby, and you turn to stare out at the view again, feeling completely at peace. He returns in minutes bearing a bottle of Veuve Clicquot and two glasses. 'I know the security detail here. The guys kept this on ice for me.'

'What would you have done if I hadn't shown up?'

He grins. 'Drunk the whole lot myself. Would've had to drown my sorrows somehow.'

He pops the cork and you both laugh as the champagne bubbles over the tops of the glasses. You clink glasses and take a sip of the frothy liquid.

You stand in comfortable silence for a few minutes, sipping the champagne. Then he takes your glass out of your hand, places it on the ledge next to you, and says: 'Okay if I kiss you?'

You nod. He takes your face in those hands and kisses you, his tongue soft and gentle, but insistent at the same time, and a lump gathers in your throat at the sheer pleasure of it.

'Shall we go somewhere more private?' he whispers.

You nod again and head for the elevator together, your hands entwined. Apart from the operator, you seem to be the only passengers. A wicked thought occurs to you as you wait for the elevator to start its descent. You tug at Firefly's hand, and he drops his ear down to your mouth. 'What if we were alone and it were to stop, right here?' you whisper.

'You mean, if someone pressed the stall button, for instance?'

You nod.

Firefly turns and says a couple of quiet words into the kindly looking operator's ear. The guy grins, then announces, 'I'm gonna take my break now. You wouldn't manage the elevator for me for fifteen minutes, would you, pal?' He tips Firefly a wink.

'I reckon I could manage that.'

The operator steps out, the door slides shut, the elevator hums downwards and Firefly presses the stall button. 'Now, what exactly did you have in mind?' he asks.

You can't believe you're being so reckless. 'Oh dear,' you say, mock-seriously. 'The lift is stuck, what will we do to pass the time?'

Firefly takes your hands, weaving his fingers between yours, and without taking his eyes off your face, he pulls you into an embrace, almost lifting you off your feet as he kisses you.

You don't know if it's the last traces of the day's excitement, or just the sheer sexy smell and proximity of him, but you've never wanted anyone more. This is your wildest fantasy playing out in real life, and you want to make memories you can play back in your mind for ever.

'I've never done anything like this before,' you say.

'Which part?' he says.

'I've never felt such chemistry with someone so soon after meeting them. And I've never shagged someone in the elevator of the Empire State Building before.'

Firefly's face lights up. 'You mean you want to ...?' Then he frowns. 'But I don't have a condom. I wasn't sure ... I mean, I hoped, but I didn't want to seem ...'

You reach into the bag Isis gave you to replace yours. 'I brought one!'

'You did?'

'Well, of course! I believe in being a grown-up.'

You kiss and kiss and kiss for an eternity, your hands in his hair, and then you move to test the ripple of his shoulders. His hands caress your back, your shoulders, and then he's pulling at the neck of your dress, pushing down your bra-straps to reach your breasts. As he drops his head into your cleavage, you run your fingernails down his back.

You fumble for his belt and unfasten his jeans, pulling down his zip, your fingertips reaching inside, then running over the quickly hardening length of his cock. His hands push up under your dress and cup your bottom as he tugs your panties aside. All restraint disappears entirely as you grab hold of his shaft in your fist, and feel him thrusting two fingers inside your pussy, pressing into the soft, hot inner core of you.

You're still clutching the condom, and you rip into it with your teeth, spit out a sliver of plastic from the packet, and then lean back against the mirror as he helps you roll it on to his cock, each of you using one hand. Then he lifts you up as if you barely weigh anything, and your heels clatter to the floor as you wrap your legs around his waist. He leans you against the mirror, his rock-hard cock pressing up against your pussy. And then he slides inside you in one smooth move and it's like you were made to fit together.

Firefly pushes into you over and over, establishing a rhythm that takes you to the edge of orgasm with dizzying speed. He spreads his legs so he can keep his balance, and hands under your bum, he turns and turns with you in his arms as he continues to thrust.

You clamp your pussy down on his cock as you get closer to coming, making him groan, and you close your eyes and enjoy the sensation of him thrusting inside you for another few seconds. Then your head spins as your orgasm explodes. Firefly staggers back, leans against the panel of buttons, and there's a clang and a whine as the elevator starts moving again. He comes with four or five last powerful thrusts as the elevator whirrs downwards, the sensation of being weightless adding to your delirium.

Still gasping for breath, Firefly lowers you carefully to the ground. You both pull your clothes back into place, panting and giggling, seconds before the elevator slows down and reaches the ground floor.

Firefly takes your hand and as you walk out together, you're suddenly acutely aware of the empty condom wrapper you've left on the floor of the elevator, silent witness to some pretty hot sex. Unless of course there are CCTV cameras in there, you think. Ah well, you're sure you aren't the first people to have had sex in that elevator, but you're pretty certain you were the most passionate.

'Well, now that we've broken the ice, how would you like to spend the rest of your visit?' Firefly says.

'I think I'd like to get to know you … again and again,' you say, hooking an arm around his waist.

THE END

You ask Isis to stay for one more drink

Isis orders you all an extra-long Long Island Iced Tea. You sip yours slowly – it's a drink that can creep up on you. Then, emboldened by the alcohol, you tell Firefly about your adventures, wisely leaving out the part about finding the air marshal sexy. He hangs on your every word, interjecting every so often to say that he wished you'd exchanged numbers so that you could have contacted him for support.

'She was brilliant,' Isis says. 'Really brave.' You share a smile. The conversation moves on to Firefly's career.

'What station do you work out of?' Isis asks.

'Rescue 1, Hell's Kitchen.'

Isis looks impressed. 'Rescue, huh?' She explains to you that Rescue 1 is the most elite company in the FDNY, and sadly lost more than half of its company during the 9/11 attacks. She turns to you. 'Your guy here has balls of steel.'

Firefly shrugs modestly, as if putting himself at risk on a daily basis is nothing special. You like him even more for this.

'Any chance we could get a tour of the station?' you ask him.

'What, now? It's past one in the morning – you must be exhausted.'

You notice that the bar has emptied out and the staff are clearly waiting for you to leave.

'I'm not tired at all,' you say. 'And besides, didn't you once promise to show me your helmet?' Isis snorts, her drink almost coming out of her nose.

Firefly shakes his head and chuckles. 'Well, I am the deputy chief. And Isis here is a government agent. I don't see why not.'

'Isis? You up for that?'

'Absolutely,' she says, draining her glass. 'Let's hit it.'

Isis hails a taxi and you all climb into the back. You're sandwiched between the two of them, their thighs pressing against yours. The taxi driver clearly thinks he's in an action movie, swinging around corners and braking too sharply, causing you to fall against Firefly. He places an arm around your shoulders to steady you, and you let him. His fingers stroke your waist, and you share a secret smile.

At the firehouse, you and Isis follow him through a side door, and he takes you around the station, which is remarkably well-equipped, with a gym and a fully stocked kitchen. A couple of beefy guys look up from the *Buffy* rerun they're watching as Firefly shows you and Isis the rec room.

'Thought you were off-duty, boss,' one of them says, giving you and Isis a quick once-over. Firefly banters with them for a few minutes, then waves you along a narrow corridor, its walls covered in notices.

He opens a door at the end of it. 'And this is where the guys can get some shut-eye.' The three of you step inside a large room with a couple of beds, a few couches and a bar fridge.

You take a seat on one of the comfy L-shaped couches and put your feet up on the well-worn coffee table. 'Don't either of you ever get scared doing this? Putting your lives on the line every day to protect other people?'

Isis takes a seat next to you while Firefly grabs a few beers from the fridge and hands them around. 'I'm so used to it, I don't even think about it any more,' Isis says. 'Ever since I was five, being a cop was all I've ever wanted. Career-wise, anyhow.' Her eyes move lazily over your body, her look laced with innuendo.

'Should I give you guys a moment?' Firefly asks, noticing the connection between the two of you – how could he miss it?

You're conflicted. There's no denying you're drawn to Isis; you can't forget how close you were to kissing her back in your hotel room. And then there's Firefly, your fantasy come to life. An incredibly hot, powerful fire-fighter, who's clearly sweet, kind, gentle, and did you mention hot?

There's a loud click and the room goes black.

'Not again!' Firefly says. 'This station is ancient, and so is the wiring. The power is always going out. There should be a flashlight, a couple of candles and some matches in the drawer under the coffee table.'

'Candles? In a fire station?' Isis asks. 'Isn't that against the regs?'

'Yeah, but what you gonna do?' he says. 'I'd better go help the guys with the generator. I'll be back as quickly as I can.' You hear the door bang as he leaves the room.

Your eyes slowly grow accustomed to the darkness, and you see Isis's silhouette fumbling for the matches and lighting the candles, which she shoves into empty bottles.

'Thought this would be better than the flashlight,' she says, her voice throaty.

She looks even sexier in this light – if that's possible.

The room is astonishingly quiet; all you can hear is the blood pounding in your ears. Isis cocks her head, an unspoken question on her lips. You're nervous and excited, but the excitement wins, and you give her a small nod.

Taking the initiative, she moves closer to you, so close that you can feel her breath on your neck. You close your eyes, and after long seconds, you feel the press of her lips on yours, the strange discovery of her soft mouth, her tongue tracing yours.

Isis continues to caress your tongue with hers, her left hand moving to cup your breast. You gasp, and mirror her touch, tentatively running your fingers down her neck and her chest. Her body is so different from the men you've been with; she's muscular, but her skin is soft and her body curves like yours. She draws the zip of your dress down and unsnaps the clasp of your bra like a professional, then runs her fingers over your naked breast, teasing your nipple between her fingers. You close your eyes, your head dropping back, both of you breathing faster ...

The sound of a man clearing his throat snaps you out of the moment. You jerk away from Isis to see Firefly standing beside the couch in the candlelight.

'I'm sorry, I didn't mean to intrude,' he says, his face flushed. 'The generator wouldn't start, Stew's working on it, should be up and running again in about fifteen. I'll give you guys some privacy …'

'No, don't go,' you say, pulling at your dress to cover yourself. There's obviously chemistry between you and Isis, but you feel the same way about Firefly. Maybe – just maybe – you can have your cake and eat it too.

'Would you stay …?' you ask, and then turn to look at Isis – she needs to be happy with what you're suggesting. 'Unless that's not cool with you, Isis?'

'Hey, the more the merrier,' she says, grabbing his wrist and pulling him towards the couch. 'O Captain! My Captain!' she purrs, as you both notice the bulge growing in his jeans.

You kneel on the couch and reach for him, and he clambers over the back to join you and Isis. You want him to feel welcome, so you take his face between your hands and kiss him, sharply aware of the intriguing contrast between him and Isis. His face is larger, harder, more angled, and there's the delicious rasp of his stubble, his tongue broader, less gentle.

As you kiss Firefly, Isis returns to your neck, kissing it and your earlobe, her fingers stroking your breasts once again. Then the three of you are tangled together on the couch, all hands and fingers and tongues, caressing, stroking, encouraging, grasping and rasping.

You lie back and close your eyes, letting the pleasure of the experience wash over you. Firefly pulls your panties down, then settles between your legs, and you gasp out loud as his mouth explores your heated pussy, searching out first your clit and then the parting between your nether lips.

Too shy to open your eyes, you feel cool air on your body as your dress is pulled right off you, leaving you completely naked. You do a tally: there's a tongue lapping at your cunt, fingers lavishing attention on your breasts, and a second tongue roving your mouth, all three parts combining to drown you in waves of pleasure.

Firefly hooks your legs over his shoulders, rubbing your clit with his thumb as he dips his tongue in and out of you again and again. Meanwhile Isis gently disengages from your mouth, drops to her knees besides the couch, and makes for Firefly's trousers. He stops what he's doing briefly to help Isis dispense with his jeans and boxers, revealing an engorged cock standing at attention.

You watch Isis as she pulls her top off over her head

in a single graceful movement, leaving her naked except for a g-string, her torso and voluptuous breasts magnificent in the candlelight.

She kneels in front of Firefly and bends to run her tongue over the tip of his cock before taking almost all of it neatly into her mouth. A guttural growl escapes from deep in Firefly's throat, and then he returns his attention to your pussy, his mouth moving up and down your slit. Hazy with delight, you can't help admiring Isis's back and sumptuous bottom alongside you as she rhythmically sucks Firefly's cock.

You reach out and run your hand over her rump, exploring the silken softness of her skin. She parts her thighs a little, and curious to know what her pussy feels like, you trail your fingers down the cleft of her bum and along her slit, which is deliciously hot and wet, alien and familiar at the same time. As you explore her with curious fingers, she nudges back against your hand, clearly wanting more. You slide a tentative finger inside her, and her pussy walls contract, sucking it in. She groans, riding your finger, so you slip another one inside her, pressing to the rhythm of Firefly's mouth on you, as he eats you with single-minded intensity, his hands on your bucking hips.

You close your eyes again, and lose yourself in sensation, and Isis pulls away from your fingers – and then she must have abandoned Firefly's cock because her lips are on yours again, her tongue in your mouth.

You hear the tearing of a condom wrapper, and then the mouth on yours is replaced with Firefly's mouth, which is pleasantly rougher and harder. There are lips and teeth on one nipple and a soft hand on the other, and the tip of Firefly's cock is rubbing up against your clit, making you arch and squirm until it presses inside you.

Now you have a hard cock filling you up, a tongue in your mouth, another on your breast. Hands rove around your body, stroking every available inch, and Firefly – at least you think it's Firefly – is clutching your haunches as he pounds into you, his skin slapping against yours, all three of you moaning loudly by now.

You grab hold of Firefly's buttocks, pulling him further inside you, wanting him to fill you up. Isis's soft hand captures yours, then places it on her mound. This time, you know what to do, and feel for the entrance to her pussy, slipping first one finger, then two, then three inside her, thrusting in time with the quickening cock inside you. She rides your hand as Firefly rides you, and eyes still squeezed shut, you heave in an orgasm that comes from so far deep inside you that it rocks outwards in waves. You feel Isis's pussy also clenching and gushing, its walls closing on your fingers like an anemone.

You gasp for air, your body slick with sweat as Firefly ramps up his pounding, jackhammering into you until he comes with a mighty shout. Then finally both Firefly and Isis collapse around you. Entirely spent, you keep your eyes closed, not wanting reality to intrude as fingers roam gently over your sensitive, orgasm-heightened skin. Fingers that could belong to Firefly or Isis, but you don't want to know who's who or what's what yet. Wait … is that burning you can smell? That was smoking hot, but surely not literally?

'Anyone else smell smoke?' Isis says.

There's a click and a pop and all the lights come back on. You blink a couple of times, realising that the room is a little hazy.

'Fire!' Isis and Firefly shout at the same time, both bounding into action as you sit gaping on the couch. Your dress must have landed on one of the candles when it was tossed aside, and fuelled by Firefly's copy of *Pride and Prejudice*, flames are threatening the base of the coffee table. There's a hiss, a sputter and suddenly, it's raining. You gasp as your naked body is peppered with icy-cold sprinkler water. The fire is extinguished in seconds, but you're in danger of going from fired-up to freezing.

'Better get you out of here,' Firefly says, lifting you from the couch and making for the door, just as four male fire-fighters burst in.

There's a moment of pure awkwardness as they take in the sight of their naked boss standing in the centre of the room, a nude woman in his arms, and an equally naked Isis beating at the last embers with her jacket.

The fire-fighters' faces run the gamut from shock to speculation and then hilarity. 'Need a hand there, boss?' one of them snorts.

'You know the rules, Captain,' says another. 'Only one person on the pole at a time.'

'It's under control, guys,' Firefly says, with surprising dignity. Still laughing and slapping each other on the back, the fire-fighters exit, and seconds later, the sprinklers sputter out.

Firefly sets you gently down on your feet, and Isis opens a window to let out the last of the smoke.

You shiver, your body a mass of goosebumps.

'Will you get in trouble?' you ask Firefly. The damage isn't that devastating, but you'll definitely need to buy a new dress at some stage.

'Nah. I'll have to put up with months of ribbing, though.' He grins. 'It was worth it. Gotta be one of the hottest situations I've ever found myself in.'

Your teeth are beginning to chatter, and Firefly reaches for a couple of jackets, placing one over Isis's shoulders and doing the same for you.

'What about you?' you ask. 'Your clothes are wet. How are you going to get warm?'

'Well,' he says, 'there's always the communal showers. The electricity may be unreliable, but the hot water is heated by gas.'

You look over at Isis. She shrugs, and then a slow smile breaks over her face. 'I'm game if you are,' she says.

'Right,' you say to your new partners in fun. 'Game on, then.'

THE END

Also in the *A Girl Walks in* . . . series

A GIRL WALKS INTO A WEDDING

Your best friend is getting married. You're going to be her bridesmaid so you have a lot to deal with – the hen party, pre-wedding nerves, your dress, the men . . . So many men. And you have to choose between them.

Maybe you'll end up having fun at this wedding after all.

* The priest is definitely heaven-sent but he's off limits, isn't he?

* Or perhaps you'll pick the best man. He's very attractive but the best man and the bridesmaid is such a cliché. Right?

* And then there's the rugged pilot – his offer of a brief encounter might have surprising consequences . . .

Whichever way you decide to go, each twist and turn will lead to an unforgettable encounter. Can you choose the ultimate sensual experience? Remember: if your first choice doesn't hit the spot, then start over and try something (and someone) new. The power is entirely yours in this fully interactive, choose-your-own-destiny novel.

Ebook out now
Paperback published in July 2014

Acknowledgements

Profuse thanks once again to Wonder Agents Oli Munson, Jennifer Custer, Hélène Ferey, and the rest of the team at A. M. Heath. We remain eternally grateful to all our publishers, especially Manpreet Grewal and her team at Sphere (Little, Brown), Amanda Bergeron and her magic helpers at William Morrow (HarperCollins), and Jeremy Boraine and colleagues at Jonathan Ball. To everyone else on five continents who keeps producing such pretty *Girls*, especially our translators, *grazie mille*, *merci beaucoup* and *danke schön*.

A very big thank-you to Zwier Veldhoen, consultant on all things Dutch, and to Clifford Hall for the guided tour of the Fragonard perfume museum at Eze, Nice. Also to André and Karina Brink for the top-to-bottom tour of the Hotel Danieli in Venice. It's not every day you get a chance to say you bounced on the Brinks' bed. We're especially grateful to Karina for helping compile a list of shag locations in the most beautiful city in the world.

And to the Usual Suspects (you know who you are): we really, truly, couldn't do it without you. Thank you all so much.

Helena S. Paige is the pseudonym of three friends. *Paige Nick* is an award-winning advertising copywriter and novelist. She also has a weekly column in *The Sunday Times*, which covers everything from sex and dating to general lunacy. *Helen Moffett* wears many hats: freelance writer, poet, editor, activist and academic, who has lectured as far afield as Trinidad and Alaska. She is also a cricket writer and flamenco fan. *Sarah Lotz* is a screenwriter and novelist with a fondness for fake names. She writes urban horror novels under the name S.L. Grey with author Louis Greenberg, and a Young Adult series with her daughter, Savannah, under the pseudonym Lily Herne.

As Helena S. Paige, these three women have created an entertaining, empowering and exciting series of choose-your-own-erotic-destiny novels, where the reader is fully in charge of her own experience. And everyone is guaranteed a happy ending.